SOMETIMES THEY SAY NOTHING
and other short stories

CHELSEA A. MOORE

INTRODUCTION

 This short story collection began as a fun thing that I posted on social media once a week. I coined the term, "short story Wednesday" where I would post stories of about 300-600 words. Some stories were ideas that were swirling in my head. Others were responses to writing prompts that were given to me or that I found onine. It was used as a healthy escape from the day to day life, allowing my mind to go to a different space for a moment. I hope these do the same for you.

 This is a thank you to everyone who read, enjoyed, and encouraged me through the initial publicity of my writing. I hope you enjoy it as much as they have!

SULLEN APATHY

Looking down at the casket, my eyes fixated on the bullet hole they miserably tried to cover up right on the left side of his neck, I couldn't help but try and force myself to be sad, but I couldn't. I guess I was supposed to be. He was my dad. God, it still feels weird to say that to this day. I was only eight years old and probably too wise beyond my years. I lifted my hand to trace his hidden wound. My mother slapped my hand between her quasi sobs. She brought her Kleenex to her nose and whispered to me, "Stop it, boy!" Low voice, but firm to make sure I did what she said. She wouldn't embarrass herself by yelling at me in public, especially at a funeral. I didn't know how long I should stare at the casket. I didn't know proper funeral protocol, so I just took a half step back and grabbed my mother's hand. I don't know why. She didn't love the man. In fact, we both barely knew him. We knew him a lot less than everyone in the room believed we did. I was looking at a stranger.

My thoughts were broken by my mom's shriek of anguish. I instantly released her hand as a reflex. By that time, she was kneeling on the ground. I looked around, silently crying out for someone in the pews to help me. My aunt and another woman came to her aid. My mother was a wonderful actress and she would milk this situation for all it was worth. Another girl about my age was standing next to my aunt. She wore a knee-length black dress with short sleeves, white ruffle socks, and black patent leather shoes, but the thing that grabbed my attention was the necklace she wore. It was an all-black locket with the initials "JS" engraved on it. I knew because I had the exact same one with "JS" on it too, my dad's initials. My hand absentmindedly went to my neck as my eyes never left hers. Our eyes met and she, almost in slow motion, reached for hers too.

"I have to go to the bathroom," she said, I'm assuming to her mom who was half listening. She motioned for me to follow her. Even at eight years old, she was bold. I followed her footsteps without telling my mom where I was going. She probably wouldn't have noticed anyway.

I followed the girl silently until we reached the front doors of the church. She walked out and sat on the steps. I sat next to her.

"We have the same necklace," I said without knowing what else to say.

"Duh, that's why I brought you out here," she said.

"My name is Savannah. What's yours?"

"Stanley."

"Hi Stanley. Is that your dad?"

"Yeah."

"Oh. My mom told me he might have other kids."

"How do you know my dad?"

"He came over to our house a lot. Usually to fix things. Our house had a lot of broken stuff."

"Oh."

I didn't really care about what my dad did when he was never home. I just wanted to know why he'd gotten her that necklace. But I didn't know if I should pry.

"You're wondering why he gave me this, huh?" she asked as if reading my mind.

"Uhhh…yeah actually."

"He wanted me to call him dad. But I didn't want to. I already have a dad. He's actually really good to me. My mom and dad got divorced."

"Oh."

She held up her hand as if to silence me. Like any sound I made would throw her off. So I shut up and sat perfectly still.

"So, I told my mom I didn't want to call him that, but she said I should do it. But I didn't want to, so I didn't."

She looked at me with tears in her eyes that she tried so hard to hold back. There was a familiarity about it. Like she'd been used to holding in tears.

"So, it made him mad. It seemed like he was mad at me every night."

"What did he do?" I asked.

She buried her face in her hands, resting them on her knees. She never answered me. Instead, she yanked the locket off, breaking it.

"He got me this the first time he hurt me. I thought he felt bad about it and he'd stop. But he never stopped. He said he'd kill my mom if I told and made me wear this every day."

She threw the locket onto the ground.

"But I don't have to wear it anymore…I know he's your dad, but I'm glad he's dead."

I sat there frozen. I didn't know what to do. I don't even know if I knew all what she meant at the time, but I knew that my dad was never there for us and was making another kid hurt. That wasn't a good man. In an effort to make her feel better, I ripped my locket off too, threw it on the ground, and stepped on it.

She smiled behind her tears. It was enough for the time. I took her hand and we went back into the church, bearing through what neither one of us wanted to endure.

THE MISSING LINK

It had been over a month since anyone had heard from Morgan Roman. I'm not sure if she tried to keep the story off the grid...unable to be traced. I assumed that's why she'd sent me a flash drive instead of just sharing it online like I asked her to do. I received the flash drive in the mail a few days after the last time I'd talked to her and I hadn't figured out what was on it yet. I tried at least twice per week over the last month and each time, I couldn't even put the drive in my laptop with my hands trembling as much as they did. So, instead, I would put the flash drive back in its envelope and put it in the kitchen drawer and preoccupy myself with something else to keep my mind off of it. "Come on, why won't you let me interview you for The Link?"

We sat in the deserted bookstore that Wednesday morning like we did every week. We'd talk about my professional development, but most importantly, the upcoming documentary I was working on: The Link, storytelling of creative geniuses of different generations. I felt like a groupie reporter rather than the student spending time with her professional mentor.

"I don't do interviews. Everyone knows that."

"Please! You're the one who encouraged me to do this documentary. How can you not be a part of it?"

Each week I tried to convince her to do it and she was being the epitome of a stubborn mule, which was definitely an understatement because I considered myself to be a pretty persuasive person. She shrugged her shoulders.

"You can do this without me telling all my business on camera. I can help you with the behind the scenes stuff."

"Yes, but having you in it would make it so much better."

"You're starting to sound like those journalists I can't stand."

Her exacerbated sigh revealed her annoyance, so I backed off a little bit.

"I'm sorry. I just thought it would be a good idea. I'm not trying to exploit you or anything. I just wanted it to be great."

I fiddled in my bag to pull out my laptop to begin talking about the logistics of the documentary. I didn't want to talk about it anymore at all, but I didn't want to be a brat just because I wasn't getting what I wanted. Morgan stared at me as I logged into my computer and it made me feel uncomfortable. I pretended not to see her and kept staring at the screen.

She sighed and said, "Ok...I have conditions."

I involuntarily shrieked, "Do you mean-!"

"Shhh...yes. We can discuss next week."

I went around the table and embraced her in a hug. I

knew it made her uneasy. She wasn't the affectionate type, but I did it anyway.

"Yeah, yeah. Just remember what I always tell you. Don't let anyone rewrite your story. And I mean that for mine, too."

That was the last conversation I had with her. She'd canceled our next meeting via text before the flash drive came, saying she would not meet with me until I'd open it. That was a month ago, until finally, I forced myself to go back to the bookstore. I sat near the window like we had done every Wednesday. I pulled out my laptop and flipped the flash drive around between my left index finger and thumb. After what felt like forever, through trembling hands I was able to get it plugged in. I opened the folder and there was only one file on the drive: *The Missing Link - Manuscript*. Was this an accident? This wasn't the content I asked for at all. I wanted an interview for my documentary, not a 200-page manuscript. Is she really going to make me read through all this content before I get my interview!? I was annoyed at the run around I was getting from her. She could have stuck with a simple "no". I wanted to grab the flash drive, throw it in the trash, and go home. Instead, I read the first page:

Keri,
Don't let anyone rewrite my story…
- Morgan

I kept scrolling down to page two...

Mary had hidden from her old lifestyle long enough. While she had enjoyed her new life, new name, and new identity as a novelist, she knew that she'd eventually have to confront the ways of her past, especially after a particular bookstore meeting with her mentee. Here she was, spouting off all the faux motivational inspiration she could find to the inquisitive young adult. She was so full of innocence, promise, and potential. Mary envied her. For at her core, she couldn't be more of a contradiction to the young woman sitting across from her. But she'd pushed that all to the back of her mind and maintained this new identity...until he spotted her. She had paranoid moments before, even though it wasn't in her nature to be paranoid, but she knew she'd seen correctly this time. They locked eyes and he left the bookstore, not without shooting another glance at her. Fortunately, he didn't have jurisdiction in her area so he couldn't arrest her, but she knew it was only a matter of time before she'd be kissing cell bars...and that's a reality she wasn't ready to accept yet. No. She would not have to confront it all just yet. She didn't want to leave her mentee behind...or any of the very few friends she'd made in her new town, but she couldn't be caught up in feelings. It was time to leave again. But it was a lifestyle she was used to...a lifestyle that began eleven years behind and 300 miles away....

It took a minute before I realized my hand had been covering my mouth the entire time and I had to remember to breathe. I took a deep breath, trying to remain as quiet as possible. I felt watched, although there were few people in the store, per usual. Was this really Morgan's story? Was her real name even Morgan? I doubted it. What was her real name? Where did she go? And what was she running from? Why would she get arrested? My mind was going a million thoughts per second, but in my hastiness, it dawned on me: I'd never read any of Morgan Roman's books. What other information laid in the other things she'd written? How much of "fiction" was truth? And I realized, I had a lot of homework to do. And it started with finishing this part of Morgan Roman's story.

THE ROAD BACK TO LENNOX

The train horn frightened me out of my sleep. It was 3:31am. The first set of early bird workers were on their way to the other side of the state to get to their jobs by 5am. Living next to the station, you'd think I'd get used to the blaring horns that came every hour at all times of night. Most days it didn't bother me, but when you're deep in sleep, communicating with your subconscious, any sudden sound, no matter how familiar, startles you. Sometimes your dreams become an escape from your reality. Other times your reality is an escape from your dreams. In this case, I wanted an escape from both. I wiped the crust out my eyes and sat up in the dark, trying to remember the details of the dream.

~

Like a ghost who couldn't be seen, I watched a reel of myself and Lenny at age 5, we were both in the sandbox and a group of kids came over to tease us. We weren't the most popular kids at the time.

"So, what kind of name is Lennox anyway?"

They laughed and threw sand at Lenny. Knowing that I'd probably be next, I did whatever I could to shield myself from the taunting. I didn't say anything. Instead, I picked up a handful of sand and threw it at Lenny too and followed it with a phony chuckle.

A few years later, we'd long forgotten about the sand incident, or at least I had, and by the time we were teenagers we'd had a ritual to go to the movies every Friday night together. While other kids at our school were getting invited to cool parties, we decided to spend that time together instead. But at 15, I'd finally gotten my first date...and it was on a Friday night.

"Are we still on for the movies tonight? I really want to see this new one!"

Lenny was obviously excited. Not wanting to break the energy, I texted back, "Sure, can't wait!"

I watched my 15-year-old self leave for my date and like a swift change of scenery, I watched as Lenny stood in front of the theater doors waiting for me, but there was no anger or sadness, just deep concern and fear.

It took us a little longer to recover from that than the sandbox incident. Three years later, I got accepted to the University of Miami, unbeknownst to Lenny. We'd agreed to apply to the University of Chicago and hopefully go together, but over-time, I wanted to go elsewhere. It wasn't an academic decision, but I was tired of focusing on studies and being an outcast and I was ready to start life anew in a sunny place.

"*What happened? I thought we were going to U of C together?!*"

"*I didn't get in,*" I lied nonchalantly.

"*You're lying! I saw the acceptance letter on the refrigerator.*"

"*Well, Len, I'm sorry. I just...I changed my mind.*"

"*Why didn't you tell me?*"

"*I didn't want to hurt your feelings.*"

"*It's too late for that!*"

Lenny stormed out the house so I wouldn't see the tears fall that were already forming. Being such a soft-spoken and caring person, it was one of the few times Lenny had yelled at me so passionately.

Even through all that, we'd always been able to get through our differences and indiscretions, except this last time.

"*I'm sorry, I didn't mean to. Can you please forgive me?*"

"*Lenny, what you did really hurt!*" I yelled.

"*I know. And I'm sorry...how can I make this right.*"

I ignored the sincere pleas.

"*You can't.*"

∿

As I replayed the events from a few months ago in my

head, I couldn't help but be consumed with all the other events I'd been dreaming and reliving that night. I missed Lenny. And although I was hurt, I'd also witnessed and had to confront all the hurt I caused. I thought of how earnest Lenny was in apologizing and how slow I'd been to do the same over the years. I thought of how quick Lenny was to forgive and how I'd turned the other way when it was my time to return the favor...that in all this time, I'd been holding onto something that didn't matter out of pride and had never realized how many times pride was set aside for me.

I grabbed my phone and began the text:

Hey, I know it's early, but I can't sleep. I've been thinking about you and I want to apologize. I'm sorry for not accepting your apology, but more than that, I haven't been the best over the years. I appreciate the great person you've been to me even when I wasn't. Can we meet up soon to talk?

I hit the send button without giving it a second glance to talk myself out of sending it. I tried to go back to sleep, but I couldn't. I laid in bed for another few hours before it was time for me to get ready for work. It wasn't until I was on the train, coffee in hand, prepared to tackle the day that I got a response:

Sure. When can you meet?

THE SMELL OF APPLE CINNAMON

"This is the last box. I can't believe you're moving out, Talia."

"Well believe it, girl. I'm so glad to move outta this apartment, I don't know what to do."

My half-sister Esme was helping me move out of Jacob's place and I was actually really excited. I couldn't wait to finally start anew and live on my own for once. We sat on the floor near the doorway and looked over the apartment. I could still smell that God-awful stench of his old track shoes mixed in with the faint trace of apple cinnamon from the Yankee candles I introduced him to.

"I guess I always thought you guys would be together forever," Esme said as she picked at the fading, dusty carpet.

"I wouldn't keep touching that carpet if I were you. Maintenance hasn't cleaned it in years."

She stopped.

"You gonna miss it?"

"Miss what?"

"Living here. Being with Jacob. I mean, you don't seem at all affected by it."

"That's because I'm just ready to move on to something new. I asked for the separation, remember? Not the other way around. I'm ready for something more mature."

"I know. I guess I just thought you would be sad or something. I mean, you were together for five years."

I stood up and dusted the back of my sweatpants.

"Esme, everyone ain't emotional like you. I'll be fine, ok. Now can you take this last box out? I'm gonna do one last sweep of the place before we leave."

I handed her the box and she sighed.

"Fine. But you owe me for all this manual labor."

She laughed and went to the car. I checked the kitchen cabinets to make sure I'd gotten all my food, checked the bathroom for all my beauty products, and then checked the bedroom for everything else.

I sat on the bed one last time and thought about this oh so great journey I was embarking on. I'd really never lived by myself before. From my parents, to a roommate, to a young marriage. I was excited and scared at the same time. I rested both of my hands next to me on the bed and just felt the touch of the sheets. I'd bought these silky sheets so we could be more comfortable at night. They were expensive, but heavenly. I should take these too, I thought.

I'd complained about this place a lot while I was living

here. The apartment was small and smelled like mold whenever it didn't smell like whatever scent the candles I bought had to offer or Jacob's torn up gym bag. The bed sat too low on the ground. The windows were too wide. I felt like other people could see everything we did from outside. Not to mention, the stove cooked my food too fast, the shower water never got hot enough, and our cable went out every week. I was ready to go.

I looked through the drawers and made sure I hadn't left anything in them. Nothing. I looked in the bottom drawer and rummaged through all of Jacob's t-shirts and socks that he would casually throw in there after wearing them if I didn't wash and fold them for him. I didn't see anything except a note at the bottom. I opened the folded piece of paper and read it.

"Dear Talia,
I know you think love letters are lame, but I'm gonna write one anyway. You make me laugh and I don't want to live with anyone else but you. I hope this letter makes you laugh too. You already know who it is, your douchebag."

All over the paper were doodles of airplanes and spaceships and hastily drawn stars. Jacob loved to draw. I remembered this letter. He wrote it and put it in my lunch bag when I wasn't looking one of the first days of us being together. I had had a bad day the day before and couldn't sleep, so he wrote it to make me feel better. Before I could stop it, my eyes filled with tears and I couldn't stop them.

I was going to miss the lukewarm showers. And the cheesy bored games we played when the cable went out. And the perfect apple cinnamon smell that covered the smell of mold and helped us both relax. And the sausages that would accidentally get burnt, but somehow tasted even better a little crispy. And the wide windows that let in the perfect amount of sunlight. Probably most of all, I would miss this bed, that sat too low to the ground, but the silky sheets made it soft and perfect, with his arm comforting me around my waist and the sweet smell of apple cinnamon putting us both to sleep.

A THREAD OF EVIDENCE

It'd been about ten years since I'd seen Claudia. We were at the mall and got separated because I just HAD to buy some pair of jeans right away and she had to use the bathroom. After making my purchase, I went to find her, but she wasn't there. At first, I thought it was another one of her practical jokes until five minutes turned to thirty. And after frantically running through the mall and eventually calling security then my mom, it was clear something else had happened.

The months and months of searches, rallies, and begging and pleading the public to help us became a frantic haze in my brain. At first, they cared. Calls poured in of different sightings, but most were dead end. Then they forgot and she became a distant memory. My dad ate his pain and depression. My mom tried to erase her existence from our lives and move on like nothing happened. The combination of their approaches didn't work for the family. The arguments between them got worse and worse. He'd survived a heart attack, but they didn't survive the marriage. But I suppose after one parent blames the other for the disap-

pearance and potential death of a child, there isn't much to recover from after that. Luckily, their official split came a few weeks
before my departure to college, so I didn't have to "choose" who
I'd live with. I just left. And they were both left with no daughters
and no spouse.

Shortly after enrolling in school, I got a job at the local
bakery. We were packed with hundreds of customers every day,
especially around breakfast, but I always noticed the regulars.
There was the overweight older man who always ordered a half
dozen donuts every single morning. I wasn't sure if he ordered
for himself or his colleagues, but that was none of my business.
He reminded me of my dad who ate himself to the heart attack
shortly after my sister left.

There was the mother of two daughters. One would come
in with her blanket every day, looking shy and the other would
skip to the counter, loudly asking her mother for a cupcake until she finally said no because it was too early in the morning
for so much sugar. The blanket girl reminded me of Claudia, the
one I'd shared a womb with, and the loud-mouthed cupcake girl
of myself, always talking over my sister and whoever else was
nearby. The only difference was Claudia didn't hold a blanket
for comfort, she'd hold a blue piece of yarn. She'd learned to do
the Jacob's Ladder yarn trick when we were seven and carried it
around with her for years after that. It was her own little blanket.
Then there was the skinny sunglasses woman. She always came
into the bakery with an older man. She wore sunglasses each time

she came into the bakery, which was once a week regularly on a Monday morning during the rush. Mondays were our busiest morning, but I always remembered her. Around 7:45, right when everyone came in before work, the man with her would order a wheat pecan muffin, our least popular item, with a black coffee. She never got anything. She would just stare blankly at me. Or at least, that's what I think she was doing. I could never be sure behind the sunglasses. She was incredibly skinny, sickly looking, and she would have a poorly cut bob haircut, inadequately styled with an old fedora. Her hair was jet black, her skin oddly pale. The older man was rude every time, demanding his disgusting muffin and strong coffee. Once I'd give it to him, he'd snatch it away and grab the woman by the waist and they'd scurry out.

One Monday, they came in the bakery and I dreaded the encounter. The man was coughing, obviously very sick and it annoyed me and the rest of my coworkers. Sick customers were bad for business.

"Welcome to Breadby's. How can I help you?" I asked, acting as if I didn't know what he wanted. This time, the woman spoke up, the man obviously too sick to even speak a complete sentence.

"He'll have a wheat pecan muffin and black coffee," there was something very robotic about her voice, yet very familiar, which was odd because I'd never heard her speak before that day. I looked her in the face to see where I knew her from. I couldn't read her look behind the sunglasses, but as the man began to cough into his napkin again, she lowered her face so I could see her eyes and said, "please."

"Umm...yes. $5.34 please."

She handed me $6 in cash because they never paid with a credit card and she said, "Keep the change."

One of my coworkers handed her the food and the man, like clockwork, grabbed her by the waist again and they headed towards the exit. I took the six dollars and began to put it in the register and stuck between the five-dollar bill and the one-dollar bill was a blue piece of yarn. I immediately looked up to see if the woman was still there and she turned and looked back at me. We both exchanged glances for a few more seconds before the man pulled on her and they both let the bakery.

~

He shoved me in the backseat and got behind the wheel. I never thought he could get any more disgusting but watching him cough and gag all day made him even more gross than I'd ever seen him. It offered me a bit of solace. I secretly enjoyed watching him suffer. Not that the minor suffering of a severe cold even remotely compared to the suffering I endured at his hands on a day-to-day basis. He wanted me to call him "Papi." Outside of interactions with him, I referred to him as, "Luci," short for Lucifer.

I was nervous as I had ever been. I'd slipped the barista a

blue piece of yarn in my last attempt to get her to recognize me. I knew my physical appearance had changed significantly over the years, but she should still be able to notice when someone was standing across from her who shared her same face. I missed my sister. Of all the things I missed, she was the one I missed the most.

It's not like Luci would know about the blue piece of yarn. I could say it got caught in my sweater and it got tangled in the money. Best case scenario, it would be a scolding, worst case, a short beating, but Luci was too sick to offer any beatings today. He shoved me in the car and said between coughs, "I need...you to...order my things for me," wiping his nose with his filthy rag, he continued, "Don't talk to anyone. Don't look at anyone...just order...give the money...and we'll leave."

The whole way there, I kept the yarn balled up in my fist. Unfortunately, he wanted to keep an extra close eye on me in his sickness, so he made me sit in the front seat.

"Do you hear me?!" was more of a command for me to respond than a question of my acknowledgement.

"Yes, Papi." I knew better than to not follow up with "Papi".

There were a few of us over the years. There was Mindy who he called Barbie because she was thin and blonde. She was his favorite, the spitting image of someone you'd see in Hollywood. He got her from a mall too. Interestingly, it was the exact same one he found me at. I sat in the car as I watched her follow willingly, a huge difference from how I'd been recruited. I'd wondered if he'd held a gun to her that was invisible to the common pedestrian. I later found out that he simply promised her a modeling opportunity and she was so attached to the idea of modeling that she eagerly went. Unfortunately, she'll never live to see that dream.

Mindy was replaced with Harper. He changed the way we both looked, cutting our hair and changing the color. He'd cut and dyed my hair and made me wear a stupid hat and sunglasses every time we went out. I guess I'd consider myself lucky. Harper could never go out. She was definitely more of a flight risk than I was. So, he took me. If the two of us were left together at home without him, he figured we might plan an escape. But he also liked to be seen with a woman in public.

Other women came and went. After his irritation with the Mindy situation, I assumed he didn't want any more dead girls. But each time one tried to escape, gave too much lip, or consistently didn't give him what he wanted, he took her on a "special date" and always returned alone. Harper made the mistake of asking where one of them had gone and it was the last time she ever did. We took beatings as a privilege around here. Beatings were warnings. He never beat women he planned to kill.

After Mindy, I became his favorite out of familiarity. He knew me and studied my motions. I was also quiet and did what I was told. Harper was way too outspoken. But she became the second favorite because she stayed and could be dominated with force, which he liked to throw around every now and then and didn't have to with me. Harper became the closest thing I'd even had to a sister after me and Cammie were separated. It was because of Harper that I decided to try and give it one more chance to get her attention. I remembered her words after I told her I'd given up trying to get her attention. I didn't want to do anything out of the ordinary and spark Luci's attention. I just always hoped that Cammie would simply recognize me one day.

"Claudia," Harper grabbed my hand breaking my train of thought, "this is our best chance. He's sick today and won't have as much strength. We may never get out of here if we don't try. Is there any way you can get her attention? Anything that she'd recognize?"

That's when I remembered I was going to be wearing a think blue sweater today that he gave me and if I could get a big enough piece from inside the sweater, it just may work.

I made my transaction and we left the bakery as normal. As Luci fumbled with the keys, I silently kept looking in the rear-view mirror. Come on, Cammie! I know you know. Trust your instincts, please! Luci coughed again and dropped his keys on the floor. This time I was in the backseat with the child lock so it wasn't like I could run out of the car. He continued to cough, and it was the first time I really wished someone would die in a moment. I could try to just hit him in the back of the head, but I'd tried fighting him before to no avail. I didn't know how weak he was in his sickness and he was already on edge from being sick as it was. I was frozen. Oh, God please!

I looked in the rearview again and saw people coming in and out the coffee shop, but no sign of the long, brown haired sister of mine...until about two seconds later I saw her run out the door. I went for broke as best I could. I took off my sunglasses and turned around so she could see me out the rear window. She glanced the parking lot until she locked on our car. *Yes! Cammie, do something. Anything!*

She picked up speed as she walked towards the car and I couldn't hold my excitement.

Luci started the car. Oh, no.

And right as he was about to back up, she knocked on the driver side window. Annoyed, he rolled down the window halfway.

"What?" He said after another cough.

"Ummm...you left your change," was all she said as she looked in the window and glanced at me.

"Didn't she tell you to keep it? Now move before I run you over."

For someone who tried to be incognito, he sure did a lot to be remembered.

Cammie stepped back as he pulled out his parking space and we began to pull off.

Really, Cammie?!

I looked in the rearview again and saw her mouthing words to herself. Then she took out her cell phone and made a call. She wasn't looking at me, but her eyes never left the back of the car. It wasn't until we'd turned the corner that I'd realized she was reading the license plate number into the phone. For the first time, I was excited to go to this place I was forced to call home and tell my friend, Harper.

~

I stared at my handwriting on the notebook and traced the letters on the paper: three letters, four numbers, on one license plate was what stood between me seeing my sister again after all these years. The positive emotions with seeing her again were short-lived as reality set in: *Who was that man? What had he done to her? What if she suffered irreparable mental and emotional damage?* She certainly wouldn't be the same person. We'd been two peas in a pod when we were kids but having to go through most of our adolescence and young adulthood in two completely different environments would almost guarantee we wouldn't know each other.

I started to feel guilty. I had more or less gone through a semi-normal childhood and often complained about it. But Claudia. Who knew what she'd had to endure? I thought of every time she'd come into the bakery and I had ignored her, trying to hurry her and her horrendous companion out the door so I wouldn't have to deal with him for another five minutes, never thinking of the woman he was with and how she had to endure him on a regular basis. And if his behavior in ordering his food at the bakery was any indication of his character, it was definitely insufferable. I wasn't sure if he had anything to do with Claudia being gone. I don't know if he was at the mall the day she disappeared, but regardless if he did or not, I knew my sister would never want to be with that kind of person. She was there against her will no matter how she got there and that automatically made him a monster.

I'd followed him the following week to his house, but I couldn't bring my legs to get out the car to knock or go in. What could I even do alone? Instead I just looked at the house, wrote down the address, and pulled off a few minutes later to avoid being seen. As much as I wanted to do this alone, I knew I'd need help. A week later, I tried to go to the police. After basically laughing in my face with what they considered insufficient evidence, they finally agreed to send a cop to the house to check things out to get me off their backs. Stupidly, I insisted I go with him. I'd driven in my own car and followed the cop to his house. The officer, Officer James, knocked on the door nonchalantly as if I was wasting his time.

"Can't you knock harder?" I asked. He ignored me. The old man answered the door just enough to stick his head out and he looked even more disgusting than all those days I'd seen him at the bakery. I wanted to pounce on him and knock out whatever life he had left, which was probably much more than it seemed. Evil, for some reason, has a way of avoiding death and overstaying its welcome.

"Yeah, good afternoon sir," Officer James said as if he was catching up with an old friend rather than looking a criminal in the face.

"What do you want?" the man asked as if there wasn't an armed officer standing in front of him. Was I in the twilight zone? The exchange was already starting off as a joke. Officer James pulled a picture out of his pocket and showed it to the man. It was the most recent photo I had of Claudia.

"We're just surveying the neighborhood, looking for a young lady who has gone missing. Have you seen this girl?"

"I ain't seen no girl!"

"Sir, can you at least look at the picture?"

He looked down for a split second and looked back at Officer James.

"Like I said… I haven't seen her."

"Sir…"

I cut him off, "I know you have her you perverted old freak! Where is she?!" I couldn't help myself. Before I knew it, I was kicking and punching the door until Officer James grabbed me and I was flailing my arms in the air like a child, screaming.

"Can I go now?" the man asked. Without waiting for a response, he slammed the door in both of our faces. I banged on the door. I didn't want to let this go without a fight.

"Open the damn door!! Let us in!!" I kept banging and banging until Officer James grabbed me again and started pulling me off the porch.

"No! He has her!" He dragged me away literally kicking and screaming until he shoved me out the gate and onto the front lawn.

"Calm down!" was all he said at first.

"I won't calm down. My sister! She…" I broke down and cried in this officer's arms who was nothing more than a stranger to me, but he was the only shoulder available.

"No one believes me!" I said between sobs.

He let me cry in his arms for a minute. After 60 seconds, I calmed down a little and he said, "That's not true. About no one believing you. I believe you."

Was he just trying to make me feel better or was he serious?

"Huh?" I looked up at him to read his face.

"I didn't at first, but that guy is…off. I'm not saying he has her, but he knows more than he's letting on."

"Then why don't you arrest him?" I didn't know if I was relieved that I had a friend in this situation or annoyed that he hadn't done anything to stop it.

"There's not enough evidence to arrest him."

"But what about-"

"The thread isn't enough. And you said yourself that the woman barely looked like your sister. And even if it is, who's to say she didn't run away from home years ago and now she's with the man willingly?"

I wanted to punch him.

"There's absolutely NO WAY-"

"I know this is hard for you to hear, but this is what it looks like in the eyes of the law."

I sighed. I couldn't believe what I was hearing.

"So, what am I supposed to do?" I asked.

"Law low. I'm going to do some digging around, but don't come back here. If you hear anything, give me call," he pulled out his card and gave it to me, "In the meantime, I'll be looking, and I'll call you with anything I find."

"Are you allowed to do this?" I didn't really care about the answer, but I wanted to know if we were teeter tottering on the illegal here.

"I'm just looking for information...for now."

"Promise you'll call?"

"Promise."

He walked me to my car and waited for me to drive away.

Three weeks had passed, and I hadn't heard from Officer James. I hadn't seen the old man again either. Every Monday he showed up with Claudia like clockwork for months until the visits abruptly stopped. I ruined it. What if my surprise visit had gotten her killed? What if he'd beaten her to a pulp because I couldn't control my anger on his doorstep? Why did I even show up with Officer James at all? Almost a month later and we were no closer to getting Claudia back, or even finding out if the woman was Claudia in the first place.

I couldn't wait until my shift was over so I could get in my car and just cry. I rushed out the employee back door at exactly 5:00. I walked as fast as I could toward my car to avoid any conversation with anyone. A few feet away from the door, I began fumbling for my keys until I was stopped by something cold sticking me in the back. I turned around and was face-to-face with the old man. The object that was in my back was now pressed against my stomach. A gun. Eyes wide, I tried to discreetly reach in my purse for pepper spray.

"Uh..uh..uh," he said wagging his free index finger from side to side. He firmly and discreetly grabbed my arm with his free hand, "Let's go." I didn't know what else to do. Here I was being held at gunpoint and my brain locked up and froze. There were no other employees, or anyone for that matter, around. He led me to his old run-down car, the one whose license plate number I'd taken down a few weeks ago. He shoved me in the back seat and slammed the door, got in the car, and drove off. I didn't know what to say or do. Or if I'd get shot in any failed attempt at escape. So instead, I just sat there.

"Do you know her?" I realized he was talking to a woman in the front seat. She turned and looked at me behind sunglasses and dark hair and simply said, "Yes." She gave me a slight smile that said she was happy to see me, but it had anguish attached to it that said she was sorry that I had come. I tried to smile back at her to let her know it would be ok, but as tears accompanied my smile, I ended up looking more sorrowful than she did. She turned back to face the windshield and I turned to look out the window next to me, neither of us saying a word the entire ride.

We'd pulled up to the old rundown house. I was right. This was where my sister had been taken. And it was my clumsy interference in my amateur investigation that landed me here with her instead of rescuing her. Before I could complete a thought, the man opened the backseat door, which I couldn't open myself because of a child lock, and grabbed my arm.

"Come on, let's go." His voice carried the gross heaviness of someone who was near death but refused to do the world a favor and die.

"Let go of me!" I tried to wrestle my arm free, but it just welcomed a punch to my face. I'd never been punched before, especially not by a grown man and the force made me so dizzy that I had to blink more times than usual to see straight again. I glanced at Claudia for a brief moment. Her expression was dry, void of any thought or emotion.

"You want to do this the hard way?" he asked me.

I didn't say anything. I just frowned at him, like a helpless child who wasn't getting their way. And that's how he saw me: a bratty child that needed to be controlled. I wanted to scream, but there was no one on the roads. No one outside. He grabbed my arm with much more power than any man at his age should have and yanked me out the car. He pushed me in front of him and placed his gun in my back like he'd done when he picked me up, "Scream and I'll shoot you." The man opened the door and pushed me inside. The first thing I noticed was the smell. It smelled like a dying animal. I coughed out of disgust. Claudia didn't seem to notice. He grabbed my arm again and began to shove me through the house. Claudia followed. We approached a bedroom at the back, dark end of the house and he unlocked the door with one of his keys. He pushed me in so hard I fell to the floor. Claudia walked in quietly after me.

"Make sure she's ready for dinner," he slammed the door and I heard him lock it from the other side.

"Oh my God...he got another one," I noticed there was another girl in the room, to my shock. Her tone didn't signify shock at my presence, but in a way, it was disappointment and I didn't know if it was at me, him, or the situation as a whole.

"She's not just another one. She's my sister." Those were the first words I'd heard Claudia say all day. She took off her hat and sunglasses and it was the first time in over a decade I got a good look at her. Her face was scrawny. Very thin in the neck. Her eyes were gray, not the usual vibrant light brown I was used to, the ones I saw in the mirror every day. She was pale and dingy like she hadn't seen any sunlight...and that's when I noticed the room. It had no windows. The one light source was a dimming lamp in the corner on top of a rusted nightstand.

I stood up and brushed the dust from my legs. "I'm Cammie."

"Harper. But it doesn't matter. He's going to rename you anyway."

"Huh?"

"He's going to give you a new name. You better answer to it. And you better call him Papi. Unless you want a knock to the face."

"Harper, stop it," Claudia cut in.

"Well, she needs to know! Better to hear it from me than experience it from him!" Harper was yelling.

"Why are you shouting?"

"Because you were supposed to get her to get us out of here! We're never going to leave!!"

"We're going to get out," I whispered.

"Yeah, that's what they all say before they end up dead!"

"No...no, really. I told a cop."

Harper gathered herself a bit and sat up, but remained on the floor, "Yeah...yeah we know all about the cop. Bet you don't know about the beating your sister took because of it."

I looked at Claudia who held her head down and walked to the other side of the room. She was avoiding me. And this other girl...she hated me. I didn't say anything. I never thought about how my showing up to the house last week with a cop, neither of us having hard enough evidence for a real arrest, would affect my sister. What was I thinking? Harper cut off my thoughts, "You're lucky she's even alive." Harper picked at the disgusting molded carpet and Claudia leaned against the wall, doing everything in her power to avoid looking at me.

"He's going to initiate you, ya know?" Harper said with a slightly more concerning tone and added, "Tonight. That's what he means by get ready for dinner. Just...just do what he says, ok? It'll be easier for you."

"What...what do you mean?"

"Don't make me spell it out for you."

"Claudia-"

I looked over at my sister. It became a bit harder for me to breathe and I tried to grab at air, hoping that what I was thinking wasn't what she meant.

"Just lay there...picture yourself somewhere else and it's usually not that bad," Harper continued.

"No!"

"It'll be over quick because you're new." Harper spoke as if she was reading from a page. It was eery. She made no eye contact as she spoke. She just stared into the air.

"I won't do it!!"

"You don't have a choice."

"No..no...no! Claudia!" I needed to hear something from her. For her to tell me it was going to be ok. That Harper was lying. That all of this was a lie and we would be going home. I knew it was selfish, but I needed something - anything - from her. But she didn't say anything. Her gaze was permanently plastered to the wall. I wasn't getting what I wanted or needed. No cops were coming to save me tonight. And there was nothing I, Harper, or Claudia could do about it.

I couldn't breathe. The room got smaller and I started to feel dizzy. "No, no, no," was all I could push out of my mouth. I dropped to my knees again from the weight that hit my legs. Between heaves, I heard the bolt on the door unlock and a second later, he came in.

"You ready, Muffin?" he asked in the creepy way where he attempted to sound sweet, but we both knew it was just condescending.

"That's not my name!"

He looked down at me quiver on the floor and spat at me.

"It is now!"

He reached for me and I found the strength to run to the other side of the room. I didn't know what I was trying to do. I was about to be cornered. He walked towards me and I swatted at him, slapping him in the face. He was barely taken aback by my weak attempts and just a second later, he pushed my face so hard that I fell back to the floor. He grabbed at my ankles and I began to kick at him.

"Get away from me! Stop!!"

I kicked at him and he let my ankles go. I tried to crawl quickly toward the door, but he grabbed my arms halfway there. He began to drag me backwards out the room. I took a quick glance at Claudia who was watching the whole thing happen from her place on the wall. She hadn't moved...but her hand was to her mouth. She was crying. Hard. It was the first emotion I had seen from her.

"NOOOO! NO!!! Let me go!!"

I wrestled with him, but it was to no avail. He was dragging me out the room and into his…

~

Every woman changes after her first night in the home. Mindy became bitter. Harper was angry. There was one girl who was psychotically laughing. She didn't stay long. She came closest to murdering Luci, stabbing him with her breakfast fork. That's when we moved to all paper and plastic meal equipment. I blocked it all out.

Cammie cried the entire night. One thing Luci did not like was women sleeping in his bed. Once he was done, he would grab the woman without a word and shove them back in the bedroom. He would go to take a shower. It was the only time he ever cleaned himself.

Harper and I would usually try and console whichever woman came, but neither of us could bring ourselves to do it with Cammie. I was too attached to her and Harper felt guilty about what she'd said earlier. I'm not sure if Cammie would even hear anything we'd had to say. When she got back, she curled into a ball in the corner of the room and stayed in the fetal position all night, sniffing silently every few minutes between quick snoozes.

We all sat in the room quietly and awkwardly until dark. Harper turned the dying lamp off a few hours later. I couldn't sleep. I stared at the ceiling as I laid on the floor. I didn't want to sleep in the bed with Harper. I didn't want to lay next to Cammie either, so I opted for the opposite corner in the room. There was nothing I could say to make this moment easier for Cammie. I'd been living through it for over a decade and it just becomes a part of the new life. It wasn't going to get any better for her if I coddled her way through it. *Gosh, I wish I'd NEVER given her that thread. She wouldn't be here. She would still be making coffees and getting muffins and doing other things that normal 20-something-year-olds do. This is my fault…*

My thoughts were interrupted by a vicious pounding on the front door. I froze and the pounding continued.

"Harper, wake up!" I whispered as loud as I could and sat up.

"What's happening?" Harper asked groggily.

The banging continued.

"Police! Open the door!!"

I ran to grab Cammie out of her sleep. Shaking her shoulder, I said, "Wake up!"

I pulled us both into the bed with Harper and huddled close. We didn't know if Luci would try and take us hostage or use one of us as a human shield from the cops as a last attempt to avoid arrest. Cammie was shaking. Harper was cursing repeatedly under her breath. Suddenly we heard the front door bang open. The three of us screamed.

"Move! Let's go!"

"Kitchen secure."

Cammie scurried off the bed and started banging on the

bedroom door.

"Help us! Please! We're in here! Oh God, help us!!"

"I hear something…" someone said on the other side.

The three of us got off the bed and started banging on the door: "Help!" "We're in here!" "Let us out!"

"They're in this one!"

"Ok, ladies. Step away from the door. We're going to come in."

We all ran as fast as we could back to the bed.

"Ok, we're away from it," Cammie said.

"Ok, one…two…three!"

The door came down with a loud crash and the three of us ran to the police officers. We didn't know where Luci was. He was likely not even home at the time. I didn't care. I was just happy that what I'd been praying for each and every day for the last decade was finally not just a dream.

≈

I couldn't sleep. It wasn't that I wasn't able to, but I really just didn't feel like I was *allowed* to. I watched Claudia sleep peacefully in the bed next to mine. We hadn't slept in the same room since we were kids. We used to beg to be in separate rooms and now we couldn't be more than a few feet apart…at least I couldn't. Claudia had remained her robotic demeanor and had said only a few words to any of us over the past couple weeks. I cried, talked, got angry, and did it all over again. Claudia lived as if it never happened by never speaking about it or anything else.

She began to toss a little in her sleep and I held my breath, wondering if this would be like every other night over the last three weeks. She paused and I exhaled deeply. I was getting by on daily naps while my mom or dad clung to Claudia during the day, but all that was starting to take a toll on me. I just wanted to sleep, but every time I closed my eyes, I saw him. Luci. The man that Claudia named after Lucifer himself. I'd found out his real name shortly after we'd finally returned home and they'd found and arrested him, but I didn't dare repeat it. He didn't deserve the satisfaction. And Claudia didn't deserve to relive it. I laid down for the first time in almost a month and stared at the ceiling in the dark.

It was hard to look at anything in the dark. What if he was behind me? Was he really in jail? I could never bring myself to read the news about it. What if he was on bail until his trial? Had his trial even started. I tried to close my eyes to stop me from thinking about it. Before I knew it, reality mixed in with my dreams and even though I was only in there for a day, all I saw was the poorly lit room with no windows. I saw his blondish gray hair. His half-wrinkled face. His powerful hands grasping at my ankles, dragging me out that room and into his. I kicked. I screamed. It did nothing. It was my first encounter with how physically inferior I was. I screamed as he closed and locked the bedroom door so Claudia and Harper couldn't escape. I tripped over my feet trying to get up and make a run for it. I was in pure survival mode and it wasn't working. I hadn't made but three steps toward the door when I was pushed to the ground for the third time that day.

"You're a fighter, huh?" he asked, taunting me.

"Let me go! Please!!" I was crying.

"Ohhh…you beg too!" he was laughing at me.

He continued to drag me towards the front of the house and around the corner. We passed the bathroom and then he picked me up and threw me on the bed.

"No!"

I tried getting up again, but he grabbed my wrists with his hands pinning me down.

"Stop!!"

He held my chest down with his knee, making it hard to breathe as he began to unbutton his shirt. I tried to push out any additional pleas that might work between heaves, but he wasn't listening. My worst nightmare was about to happen, and it had already happened to Claudia, probably on a regular basis.

"No..No!! Please!" I shouted at the top of my lungs when he finally lightened the pressure from my chest.

I was awakened by a hand on my shoulder. I was hot. Sweating. It was hard to breathe, and I worked hard to catch a bit of air.

"Here."

I was handed a bottle of water. That helped and I was able to resume regular breathing after a couple more swallows. I leaned on the shoulder that was next to me. Thinking it was my mother, I hugged her tightly, but feeling the skinny waist, I realized it wasn't her. It was Claudia.

"The nightmares are worse at night," she said. She had spoken more to me in that sentence than she had in the last few weeks. She caressed my hair while I laid on her shoulder. Who was this woman that was so brave? She'd endured my one traumatic day every single day for ten years. And yet she was the one consoling me.

"You know...we wouldn't be here if it wasn't for you bringing that cop," she said plainly.

"I should've recognized you sooner," I replied. I didn't feel like a hero or anything. I felt guilty and ashamed.

"You weren't supposed to. He made sure of that...and I could've spoken up sooner. But we didn't. And it's ok. We're here now." There was no optimism in her voice, but no pessimism either. It just was what it was, like reading facts from a textbook.

We sat in the dark together until we both fell asleep next to each other. While I knew we had a long way to go, I took the night for what I could. It was the first night we'd laid next to each other. And it was the first night we actually slept.

HIGH TIDE

It was 2:37am and like morning mist, his presence had slowly evaporated from her as her eyes gradually recognized the change of scenery. His touch, his scent, his voice had been all too familiar. Way too close as if he was lying next to her. How could something as fleeting and unreal as a dream seem so close? She could still feel the touch of his lips on hers. She wasn't sure whether to be grateful for the experience or cry that it has passed. Tonight, she chose to cry. Through sleepy eyes, tears streamed down her face. She didn't dare check her phone for a missed call or text. She knew it wouldn't be there.

She'd wondered if he'd been thinking about her too. Wondered if the distance was tearing him up as much as it had been doing to her. She almost laughed at herself for how melodramatic she was being. It wasn't in her nature to fret, but that's certainly what her mind was doing. She thought of all the mistakes she'd made. All the misunderstandings, all the times she didn't trust him, all the miscommunications. All the times she hid how much she cared. All the times she had one foot out the door. How she never gave the benefit of the doubt. How she never trusted him...or anybody. For being difficult. For not living up to what she'd promised. For all around being scared...for all she'd done to him in contrast to all he'd done for her.

I'm sorry. I really am. She hoped he could hear her thoughts. That somehow in all of him knowing her, he would know this. But as hard as she hoped, she knew it would be to no avail.

She closed her eyes and rolled back over in the dark, trying desperately to get a taste of the dream back. She tried to smell the mist from the lake. Feel his arms around her again. Hear his voice whisper in her ear, "I love you" and for once, she'd say in return, "I love you too" as they both cherished the embrace and watched the waves kiss the pier at high tide.

A RICH EXPLORATION

"You sure know how to get a room excited."

David's husky voice scared Rima. She had been staring at the mountains in the distance from her balcony for nearly twenty minutes with barely a movement, except for the occasional switch to shift her weight from one leg to the other.

"Oh," she looked down at her feet, mainly to avoid the eye contact.

"You're not cold?" he asked.

"No, not really. This view is amazing. It helps me think, too."

She paused, then continued, "If I'm going to tell everyone else to come here and get the answers they're looking for, I'm going to have to do the same for myself, huh?"

"Yeah."

The rest of the crew were inside drinking beers and playing games. Rima didn't know if the trip was fulfilling its purpose or not.

"Don't worry so much about this trip Rima. People are

taking what you said seriously. Ella already called James and broke it off. Damien and Eric both applied for new jobs today. Ari applied to culinary school...and those are only the people I've talked to today."

Rima lit up at that and let out a sigh of relief.

"I'm glad everyone else has the courage to do it. But I'm not even sure where to start for myself."

David went to stand closer to her on the balcony as they both looked towards the mountains.

"Well, you said you wanted to do music, right?"

"Yeah."

"Well...I have something for you."

He reached into his coat pocket and pulled out a card.

"What's this?"

"Give this woman a call. I know her personally. I already put in a good word for you. She works in the admissions office at the VannHouse College of Music."

"David, that's like the best music school on this side of the country."

"Exactly."

"I can't go." She tried to hand the card back to him.

"Rima...you said you wanted to do this. You should do it."

She thought about it, but she couldn't think of her dream without her father's words attached to it, *"There's no real money in music unless you want to take drugs with it and if you think I'm going to help fund that, you have another thing coming!"*

Just twenty-four hours ago she was the woman of the room and now she didn't know if the very words she'd spoken to the crowd of people were something she could support.

～

"Ok, ok everyone. I know we're all excited, but let's circle up for a bit," Rima gathered the cabin room of almost 30 twenty-something-year-olds to order. She stood on one of the tables and everyone turned their attention to her.

"You guys ready to hit the slopes?!" she shouted. She was met with the room duplicating her excitement.

"Ok, ok. Let's pipe down for a minute. Now, I think we all know this trip is about more than just skiing. We're all adults, but living this life, you never really get to get out of your parents wings, am I right?"

She was met with nods and cheers of agreement as if she were a preacher being encouraged by his congregation. She lifted her hand and smiled to calm them down again.

"I brought you all here because I want you to have fun, but more importantly, I want you to figure out what you want to do. Most of us are at a college we don't want to be at, studying a subject we don't want to make a career of. Some of you are going into a family business you have no interest in. And a few of you are in relationships to appease your families. Now's the time to figure that all out. What does the person in the mirror want?"

She let the question linger in the air. Then continued, "We've been blessed and lucky enough to have money."

The room cheered some folks high fiving each other, but she silenced them, this time without a smile. "BUT we know that sometimes that's a curse more than a blessing." This time she was met with somber murmurs of agreement. She perked the room back up and finished, "But we're going to gain control of our lives this weekend! So, let's have fun!" The room gave one last cheer and began to gather their luggage and headed to their respective rooms.

$$\sim$$

"Rima, you brought us all these miles away to tell us to get away from the words of everyone else and listen to our own. You can't tell us that and then run away in fear when you have to do it yourself."

She let out a stressful sigh.

"Will you help me?"

"Of course, I already started by giving you the card, didn't I?" he said and they both laughed.

He looked at her and admired this woman who, although young, was so much smarter and more powerful than she even realized. She would be amazing at any career, really, but he knew her life wouldn't be complete if she didn't explore her love for music, whether that's what she ended up doing in the long run or not, she needed the freedom to know. The freedom to explore. And he'd help her get there if she let him.

She glanced over at him and he sensed her discomfort at the attention.

"Why are you staring at me?"

He didn't answer her. He just grabbed her chin and kissed her lightly, just letting his lips graze hers. Because although he had hounded her about figuring out what she wanted to do with music and she hounded everyone else to do what they needed to for their own lives, he needed to do the same for himself: to explore the type of woman his own father disapproved of, the type of woman who voiced her opinion and encouraged others to do the same rather than sheepishly following orders like his mother. And he knew with the way she kissed him back that she would let him explore them, just like he'd help her explore her music, no matter how the two would end up in the end.

AN UNFAMILIAR LEGACY

They say the non-religious only go to church for funerals and weddings, and honestly, for me, even that is too often. I pulled at my dress that one of my aunts would think is too short, but hopefully they would be too preoccupied to comment on it. As I made my way out of the car and into the church, I knew there was nowhere else I'd rather be than in that ocean. Hell, I'd even take a dirty pond than to go inside. Most people travel to bodies of water to escape, to relax, to get away. For me, it was an adventure, a different escape of sorts, no matter how calm or raging the water was.

There weren't many people I was happy to see except my sister Camillah. She ran up to me as I got out the car and said, "Boy am I glad to see you!" She tugged at me, prepping me for the unholy reunion of our family, how I should still make conversation, so I won't look like the family snob and how she'd said all good things about me to halt some of the gossip.

After unbearable small talk and chatter with family I hadn't seen in years, I sat and stared at the woman in the casket and could not muster up any sadness or tears. Had I really become that bad of a person? I'd visited my grandmother often when I was a child, but once I became a teenager, that slowed down. It was non existent in my adulthood. She called me every now and then, but more often than not, I missed her phone call. Sometimes it was on purpose. Sometimes I was just too busy and couldn't remember to call her back. She did always leave a voicemail saying she loved me and hoped to see me soon, but I'd never made it back home in time to do that. Even still, I felt nothing, looking at her lifeless body.

Was Aunt Ella right that my lack of faith and escape from our conservative town had caused me to become a heathen? Or maybe Aunt Josephine was right in saying that I had become a different person (and not for the better) after escaping to a hippie liberal city to become a beach bum oceanographer? It didn't matter how many times I tried to tell her, or the rest of the family for that matter, that I didn't live on the beach. I was actually rarely ever on it and there was a difference between an oceanographer and a marine biologist. They didn't want to hear any of it. Once a rumor started in the VanHouston family, it became etched in stone as truth.

The preacher opened the floor for people to make comments and this was the part I hated most about our family funerals. There were the relatives that endlessly told stories. There were the family strangers who swore they were close family friends. These people usually made the greatest spectacle, spending more time loudly crying than actually giving a coherent speech of substance. There were people who would come up to say one or two words and maybe cry silently afterwards. These people were sincere, but rarely was what they had to say necessary.

And then through all that garbage to sift through, you may be lucky enough to have that one person that gave a great speech: not too short, not too long, something that not only gave insight into the person whose life we were celebrating and mourning, but also would give some insight into the lives of the people in the audience. Nothing cliché, not too deep, but the perfect mixture of both sorrow and peace. And over the years, while the rest of my family would gossip about how terrible everything else was, I could sit in silence holding onto whatever small token I could find in the rubble.

"Is there anyone else who would like to say anything on behalf of Mrs. Edna VanHouston?"

Oh, God, I wanted this to be over. There were a few murmurs in the audience, but everyone who wanted to say anything had already spoken...except Camillah. She stood slowly, holding her head down and comforting her right arm with her left hand, while carefully walking to the microphone. It was weird seeing her like this. Cammie isn't shy, but she's no public speaker either so the whole sight made me feel like I was looking at a stranger. In fact, I couldn't feel more lost and alone with people I've known since birth than I did at that moment. It got really quiet before she started as everyone anticipated what she would say.

"Ummm…" Cammie was cut off by feedback in the microphone that made her take a step back. It through her off a little. Please, don't let her mess this up.

"Sorry," she cleared her throat and I saw her natural boldness begin to come back.

"Many people know this woman as Mrs. VanHouston or Aunt Edna…but for me she was just Gammie. My mother used to tell me that when I was three, I couldn't pronounce 'grandma' so I'd call her 'gammie.' I've been calling her that ever since." She was met with a few chuckles in the audience. That made her smile.

"A lot of people talk about how Gammie was really into her faith. How she would pray for everyone…or how she would volunteer at the women's shelter. Or how she was a great mother to her five children. Yeah, she was all those things…but most people don't know who she was behind closed doors too. Five years ago was the hardest time for my sister and I, as many of you already know. We lost our dad…then shortly after, our mom left. I'm proud of my sister. She pressed on and did what she needed and wanted to do for herself and her career. I was so happy for her, but in a way, I was sad because I didn't know what I wanted to do, and I didn't have my best friend next to me. That's when I moved in with Gammie. I'll admit at first, I didn't want to. I was 19 and definitely wanted to do my own thing."

She said it in a way that caused everyone to laugh with her again. It lightened the mood a bit from her bringing up two elephants in the room: the death of our father and the voluntary disappearance of our mother.

"But, while I expected Gammie to be strict and harsh, instead she just loved me. I couldn't decide what I wanted to say in front of you all today. I was going to talk about how she taught me how to bake a cake and drive a stick shift and how to knit and salsa dance and change a tire...but that's not important. All those things I could've learned on the internet. In those moments, she gave me what I could never get from a Google search. Like how we talked and cried for hours about my mother, who wasn't even her biological daughter, while baking that cake. And how she let me know it was ok to eat an extra piece as long as it didn't become my permanent way of comfort. Or how she taught me to beat the odds and defy social norms while teaching me to drive a stick shift, which she learned at 60 years old! Or how she showed me how to have peaceful moments, while teaching me how to knit. Or when I was depressed, she picked me up and showed me some fun while salsa dancing in her living room. Or showing me that it's ok when life gets heavy and dirty while teaching me how to change that tire. And the many, many nights she let me sleep in her bed or on the couch together, never telling me she had a bad back, but letting me get the comfort I needed. I think the best thing about Gammie is, she wasn't just this person with me, but with everyone she encountered. And in her death, I can only hope that I will help carry her legacy and be at least half the person to others as she was to me."

The room fell silent as she wrapped up, "I love you, Gammie. I'm gonna miss you. Thank you...for everything."

Camilla received a standing ovation, with majority of the audience applauding and wiping tears from their eyes. I couldn't stand. I wanted to, but I was frozen where I was. I didn't know what to say or do, or even if I should. In that moment, I felt exposed. Like all my misgivings were on display even though no one was looking at me. The family drama and bickering and gossip didn't matter at all. What mattered was that the person that my sister needed at her most precious time of need was there when no one else was. She was this person for her and many others in the room.

I regretted not being there for my sister. I regretted escaping from her and this family. I regretted not checking on her to see if she was ok. And most of all, I regretted not allowing Edna VanHouston to be that for me. Better yet, I regretted not being anything for her, but writing her off with everyone else and never giving her a chance when she never wrote me off, as she probably should have. I tried to stand, but I couldn't. For as soon as I did, my knees gave way and I was leaning over the pew in front of me. The tears I'd been holding over the past five years had suddenly come out all at once. I don't know how long I was crying. I just felt an unfamiliar pair of hands touch my shoulders. They stayed there until I was done. And when I could finally get the words out, all I could say was, "I'm sorry, Gammie."

BLACKMAILED

"My wife says I'm selfish. But aren't we all just a little bit selfish doctor? Wouldn't you agree?"

The monotonous tone of his voice let Dr. Erica Hansen know all she needed to know. She couldn't figure out how he had gone so long without getting locked up. Instead, he was sitting in her office for an analysis. Only fifteen minutes into the conversation with Jackson Morgan, she already knew what her diagnosis would be. At face value, and to the untrained eye, most people wouldn't see him for the psychopath that he was, but Dr. Hansen was good at what she did, and she could spot one from a mile away.

"Mr. Morgan," she adjusted her glasses as she let out a deep breath.

"Please, doctor. Call me Jax, I've told you before," he said in that faux friendly tone. He got up to pace the room. Dr. Hansen allowed it. Jax was the type who needed to feel like he had some type of power to thrive.

"I know you want to write on your little pad about how

crazy you think I am... or maybe how handsome," he followed with a chuckle. Dr. Hansen was not amused. He continued, "But you're going to let me go. You're going to tell them that I'm perfectly fine and let me out of here. And then we can move on with our day and put this behind us."

"And why would I do that Mr. Morgan?"

He pointed at her and smiled.

"I've done my research on you, Doctor. And I've been excited to meet you. I'd consider us friends, wouldn't you? You can help me. And I'll help you."

"And how could you possibly help me?"

He walked slowly back to the table and took his seat directly across from her.

His voice went down, to a hollow whisper, "Now...you wouldn't want people to know what really happened to Jared... would you?"

∾

"Stop trying to diagnose me! I'm not one of your patients!" The familiar conversation replayed in her head as she twirled the ring on her left hand. Jared was getting worse, but there was no convincing him of that.

"Hey E!" her thoughts were cut off by one of her colleagues.

"Hey Dani."

"Why so sad? You alright?"

"I'm fine."

"No, you're not. What's going on?"

"Jared."

Dani's face fell from its usual perky self. Dani knew all the assorted details about Erica and Jared.

"Has he considered seeing someone?"

"Come on, D. You know he won't do it."

"Have you tried telling him-"

"I've tried saying everything in every way I know how. He's not doing it."

She tried to be polite, but the frustration was showing in her voice.

"What about medication?"

"You know he can't take medication without a diagnosis and a prescription. Besides, he feels the same way about medicine that he does about seeing a doctor. He wouldn't take anything even if I offered it."

"Yeah but using alcohol as medication isn't helping him either."

"Don't you think I know that?"

They both sat in silence for a few moments.

"I'm sorry, E. I just hate seeing you like this. It's starting to take a toll on you."

"He hit me last night, Dani. He's never done that before. He-"

Erica buried her head in Dani's shoulder. She didn't know if any of her other coworkers were seeing or hearing any of this as they ate their lunches, but she couldn't keep it in. Dani patted her back and let her cry for a moment.

"You have to get out of that house."

"I just want him to get better."

"Then you'll have to do what you haven't done."

"Like what? I'm out of options. I feel desperate."

"Then you'll have to do something desperate."

Erica sat up and looked at her friend.

"What do you mean?"

"He needs treatment. What if...what if he doesn't know he's getting treated?"

"Are you saying I should compromise my career and-"

"Shhhh...I'm not saying anything. I'm just saying...do what you have to do."

A week had gone by and he'd stormed out of the house again. Erica watched from the window, pack of ice to her face to bring the swelling down of her freshly bruised cheek, as he stumbled into the driver seat with his bottle in his hand and swerved out of the driveway. Maybe she shouldn't have taken Dani's words so seriously. But in her desperation, she didn't anticipate how much drinking he'd do that night.

"Ok, here you go," Dani hurriedly told her before he came home. She'd transferred the pills into two plastic bags for easy hiding.

"Just two is enough."

L   *ittle did Erica know, Dani meant two as in one of each,*
not two of each. In her haste in making dinner, she chopped up
four total tablets and threw them in with Jared's food. Was it too
much? She'd prescribed medications to people all the time, but
rarely paid attention to the dosage. That was the patient's respon-
sibility in reading the label. She'd paced the floor all night, nurs-
ing her discolored cheekbone. She'd fallen asleep for a half hour
right as the sun was rising and woke up to an abrupt banging on
the front door. When she opened the door, she was greeted by
two police officers.

～

"Now, everyone is saying it was a drunk driving accident.
Open and shut case. But the toxicology report is kind of interest-
ing--"

"Stop!"

"I think it's also pretty interesting that those same drugs
were prescribed to your former colleague, Daniella Boyers..who's
never had any history of anxiety or depression. Weird."

He scrunched up his face, simulating genuine confusion.

"I said, stop."

"Best case scenario, you lose your license. Worst case...I
wonder how many would consider this a murder? I mean...he
was kind of abusive, right? You definitely have a justified motive."

He glanced at her.

"Ah, don't worry. I'm sure a jury would side with you."

He looked her in the eye and couldn't keep the smug smile off his face. He got the kind of satisfaction of checkmating an opponent in a game of chess.

"What do you want?" she whispered through clenched teeth.

"Tell them nothing's wrong with me...and your secret will be safe with me."

She didn't say anything for a moment. Then closed her notebook.

"This session is over."

"I rather enjoyed our talk, Dr. Hansen. Maybe we can do this again sometime," he said as she was walking out the door.

"So, what do you think? He's dangerous, right?" Erica jumped at the sound of a woman speaking to her as she came out of the room. The woman looked scared. Dr. Hansen turned to her boss, who was standing next to the woman.

"Cut him loose."

The woman inhaled and lightly gasped in fear as a tear trickled down her cheek. Erica looked at the woman's hand and noticed a ring on her left hand and could only pray the woman's situation wouldn't turn out like her own.

CITY SENSES

The smell of freshly made funnel cakes always matched the way they tasted: warm and sweet. As a girl, it always enveloped me during our annual trip to Kings Cavern, the local amusement park in Arbor City. While my brothers always wanted to get on all the roller coasters, I just wanted to get all the overpriced snacks: hot dogs, DippinDots, but most of all the funnel cake. I was too afraid to get on any rides and being the baby and only girl of the group, I just flashed a smile to my dad, kissed his cheek, and I always got the funnel cake. Even though we only lived about thirty minutes away from Kings Cavern, it was always a big annual trip, the one time in the summer where my mom, dad, and three brothers could be together at once and do something great. I'd eat my sugar and rub my palms against my dad's beard and that was enough for me.

The funnel cake didn't compare to the French Dip sandwiches at The Uptempo restaurant, a place and sandwich I only began to appreciate once I noticed that the funnel cake was mostly smell and not much taste. But the French Dip sandwich was different. Although it didn't smell nearly as good as Kings Cavern, the salty, oily, savory flavors always lit a little fire and began a party in my taste buds. Kings Cavern came second to Uptempo. Kings Cavern was a day full of adventure, but it was always only one day per year. Uptempo became a weekly tradition in our house.

"You know, you really shouldn't eat all that beef, honey," my mom would scold me.

"Ahhh, let her have it. It's a treat!" my dad would retort for me. My dad and I weren't lucky like my mom to be able to eat what we wanted and still stay slim. If it wasn't for the military, he'd be twice his already husky size. He'd playfully mess with my hair, moving my bangs out of place when he said it. And I couldn't help but smile every time, carefully smoothing my hair back in place and going to the counter, "One French Dip Sandwich, please."

Our family exchanged The Uptempo tradition for what I like to call, "Everyone Does Their Own Thing" phase and I developed a tradition of my own. This time it didn't involve the smell of sweets or the taste of beef, but the touch of boys...one in particular. Taking my oldest two brothers to college, with my dad being in different states for months at a time, caused for a virtually empty house. The playful kisses, hugs, and affirming words left the house with my dad and brothers.

The boy's name was Arden. I was fourteen at the time and wasn't into dating as much as my friends...until he showed up. Two years older than me and so much more mature (in my mind). Hockey was the sport in Arbor City. We'd go to watch his brother play every week, running into locals in the city and classmates from school. I'd grip his hand and interlock our fingers, loving the sensation of a simple hand hold, but also secretly enjoying this public display of affection that said, "I'm good enough to publicly be this guy's girlfriend." After the game, we'd wait for his family in his car and sneak in quick teenage kissing. "I'm making out in a car!" was all I would think and break our kisses with my giggles. He'd break my subsequent feelings of embarrassment and insecurity by touching my chin and looking me in the eyes, and as if reading my mind would say, "It's ok," followed by a laugh of his own.

He was a place of solace at that time for me, when I'd find myself in a bickering match between my mother who was mourning her emptying house, or my brother who I rarely got along with because I'd stolen his spot in the family as the youngest, during the week. I eventually kept to myself, always silently waiting for that Friday night Arbor City hockey game.

When I was 17, I made the decision to be like my dad and go to the military, against my mother's stern wishes. I told her one day when my dad returned home to soften the blow.

"Guys, I've decided what I want to do after high school is over."

I saw them both light up with intense anticipation.

"I want to go to the military like Dad."

The looks on both of their faces couldn't be more of a stark contrast. My dad lit up with excitement. I'd never told him I was thinking of following in his footsteps because I wanted to make the decision on my own. My mom, on the other hand, could not be any angrier and she wasn't shy about vocalizing it.

"That's a horrible idea!" She then turned to my dad, "You! You did this!" she started yelling accusations at him, shoving him outside the kitchen as he shielded his face from her flailing arms. They'd been arguing and screaming so much throughout the rest of the day that we'd missed the Red Flag Warning. My mother ran into my room at 3am, shaking me out of my sleep.

"Let's go. NOW!!"

"What? What's happening?" I wasn't sure if I was dreaming or not.

"Fires! Wildfires! We have to go!"

I ran out of my bed, wanting to take some of my things with me, but my mom grabbed my arm and yanked me out of my bedroom. We piled in the car in our pajamas with nothing to carry with us. It wasn't until I sat in the car that I'd seen the sky, lit up like lava, the smoke resembling heavy storm clouds. There was something apocalyptic and eerily peaceful about it at the same time. I watched in the rearview as we pulled off, seeing the fire in the distance, but knowing that the distance meant nothing at a time like this. That peaceful apocalypse was only peaceful from a distance and that view would be replaced about a week later with misty remnants of smoke caressing the ashes and debris that stood where our home used to be.

The Uptown went down with the many other buildings. The hockey team was relocated to Middleton, the next city over. What Kings Cavern didn't take in a physical hit, they took in a financial one, which caused them to permanently close about a year later, but how can you make money in a place where there are no more citizens? Like many others in Arbor City, we took up residence in Middleton. Our little neighborhood had many of the Arbor City locals to move in and Middleton became a place to hear all the stories of the "good ole days" in "The City".

I spent my last few months before moving out stopping at local coffee shops, bookstores, and parks to listen to what people were saying. Most people didn't say much, but every now and then I'd catch conversations reminiscent of the city: seeing the fireworks on the fourth of July, touching the animals at the petting zoo, tasting the food at the food truck festival, hearing the live music during the summer concerts, smelling the scented Christmas trees during the annual tree lighting. And although I had participated in all those things too at some point, I knew the memories I held closest to me were the ones that included the one person who could really only be there half the time. As I prepared to follow in his example, I held nothing against him for his absence. I silently thanked him for giving me what he could in Arbor City.

BLISSFUL IGNORANCE

Bella said my job had made me emotionless. A bit harsh, but I'm sure there was some truth to it. Once you find out people's deep secrets and realize they sleep just fine at night despite of it, it changes you a bit. First it bothers you. Then you realize you have to either become numb to it or quit. I had debts and bills to pay so quitting wasn't an option. For eight years, the job had its ups and downs. One of the ultimate downsides was my relationship with Bella.

"Tell me you care," she pleaded with me.

"I do care!" I responded but couldn't look her in the face. I hated seeing her like this. She was breaking and I was causing it, chiseling away at her with every word I spoke during the conversation, telling her I didn't want to give what she needed. But I had to be honest, "Maybe just not enough," I said in a whisper to soften the blow, but the tone didn't matter. After four years, we just couldn't give each other what the other wanted. She was ready to move our relationship to another level and I wasn't. And I cared about her too much to continue stringing her along. I know now that it was my own fear and insecurities that caused us to part ways and that's something I'd have to live with. I wanted to forget about it and scrub my history clean of her, but it never quite worked. With every job I took after that, I contemplated whether what she said was true. I denied it for years, but there was one job that made me realize she might be right.

I'd received an email like any other. An employer was suspicious of his employee embezzling funds and needed some investigating before getting the police involved. Sure. I'd done this kind of thing before. Easy money. But once I'd received the man's name and photo who I'd be investigating, my heart dropped a little. David Pearson. The last thing I needed was for my job to get messy. And that's exactly what would happen if I didn't handle it with delicacy. David Pearson was Bella's new boyfriend turned fiancé. I'd only known through Facebook. I never reached out to say congratulations or anything and she never told me. Maybe it's best she didn't. We were more or less strangers at this point.

I took the job anyway and most of it was boring surveillance work, which was typical of a job like mine; just watching and waiting until some break or some piece of evidence came to kick the investigation into high gear. After two weeks, it finally came. I followed David to a downtown bar. For the morally upstanding, white collar, family-oriented American man he painted himself to be, he sure drank a lot. I worried if I could keep following him to this bar before he'd notice, but after a few beers, the guy didn't even know his own last name. I wondered if his family or employers knew about his obvious alcohol problem. But I wasn't hired to discover whether or not he was an alcoholic. That would be just gravy to the meal I was looking to find.

The night went like every other night for the last two weeks: watching David drink and talk to the bartender until he got enough courage to talk to other strangers at the bar. Once he was really plastered, he'd go to the women. This night, however, there was one woman in particular that he took special interest in. She, not as drunk as he was, but certainly not sober, laughed at all his corny jokes and playfully touched his arm. It was disgusting. After an hour of watching this unbearable show, they both got up. She helped carry him out of his chair and they left. I didn't know what they were going to do. This wasn't an infidelity case and I wasn't hired to find out if he was a cheating scumbag, even though that ship sailed a long time ago. No, I was interested in the wallet he left behind.

David was so busy chatting with the woman that he didn't realize he'd left it. Quickly, I grabbed it and excused myself to the bathroom. Looking through it in the stall, nothing was out of the ordinary at first. Just an ID and some credit cards. But then I opened the back flap and there was the major clue that nailed him: another ID with his picture on it. He looked at least ten years younger. "Why would he keep an old ID?" I asked myself aloud. Maybe he'd forgotten he had it. The reasoning didn't matter, but the name on it did. It didn't say David Pearson, but a new name: Craig Hollandsworth. This is when my job got interesting and my adrenaline would kick in. I wrote the name down and handed the wallet to the bartender to keep in the lost and found.

It was too late to call my client, so I decided on a simple social media and Google search instead. The internet made the job of private investigators so much easier sometimes. "Ok, he went through a name change. That's usually not a good sign," I said to no one in particular. My research took me through the rest of the night. Craig had been imprisoned for embezzlement and served five years for his crimes some 300 miles from here. After his release, he had other similar charges against him, but none ever stuck. His rap sheet ended around the same time David Pearson appeared in this city. It didn't take a genius to figure out what he was doing. I hadn't proved that David/Craig was stealing from his current job, but I'd had enough information to consider this a job well done. Lying about his history and name change was enough to at least get him fired and then his job could do a more thorough search into things that I didn't have access to. Case closed. My job was done. As much as I wanted to wipe my hands clean of it, there was one thing that still lingered in the air. The same thing that came to my mind after most cases. *Am I emotionless? Why don't I care about this or anyone else this is going to affect?*

I couldn't get Bella's words out my mind. I didn't know if it was her or her words that had impressed on me so much, but after that case, I needed to know. I sent her a message on Facebook and asked her if I could talk to her. She respectfully declined, saying it was a "bad time", that the wedding date was in a week and she'd had way too much to do. And anyway, "we don't really have anything to talk about" and she had "no hard feelings" but I was "more than welcome to come to the open ceremony". Pfft. Her candid response actually took me aback. I didn't like it. I went to the ceremony anyway. I'm not sure why. I never ended up talking to her. I just watched as she came down the aisle, looking happy and gorgeous and ready to be Mrs. Isabella Pearson. Except she had no idea that she was really marrying Craig Hollandsworth: the lying, stealing, cheating alcoholic. I can't say I wanted her back. I didn't know. There was just a slither of tension inside me I couldn't quite articulate. The tension that knew that even though this was the happiest day of her life, she probably wouldn't remember it fondly, that because of the work I'd agreed to do, she'd be lucky to get through the honeymoon phase. The tension that knew in the best-case scenario he'd lose his job and the worst, but most likely case, he'd be in jail. And all the planning and money spent on flowers and dresses and pictures and food and rings would all be for nothing. That, again, somehow, I'd managed to cause her pain and damage and loneliness. The worst part was, I didn't feel as bad as I wanted to about it. Because if I could do it all over again, I still would do it the same way. That even though I was exposing truth, I was also crushing hearts when most people would prefer to live in obliviousness. Bella was one of those people and I would rip her apart with truth yet again. Maybe Bella was right, and my job had made me emotionless. As hard as that was to accept, now wasn't the time to ponder it. Right now, I just watched them smile at each other and recite their vows. Her life would change for the worse soon enough. But today, she could live in her joy and blissful ignorance until the truth came and shattered it all.

BUCKET HIT

I met Rhonda at the local park trail: a typical, outdoor space. It was crisp and breezy in the early autumn morning air. She went every morning to jog. She had a very predictable, typical single middle-aged woman lifestyle, far from the drug-addicted slum her ex-husband made her out to be. It was probably a lie, but that had nothing to do with me. I jogged that fateful Wednesday and "crashed" into her on the trail.

"Oh my God, I'm so sorry," I exclaimed.

"Oh, no it's alright. Sometimes I get so caught up in my run I don't notice anyone around me."

It was so easy to talk to people. They left so many doors open for conversation.

"Tell me about it. I do too…except I'm new to this trail." Of course, I had to leave the door open for her too.

"Oh, I run this one all the time. It's usually pretty crowded with families at this time. School letting out, you know?" she said pointing to the children.

"Yeah I see. But that's why I like it. My old trail was deserted, and it got kind of lonely. I like to feel like I'm working out with other people, even if they're not really working out with me. It's silly," I said in the kind of way that I knew would make her feel sorry for me.

"Well, hey, I've been jogging by myself for a while after I left my horrible ex-husband," she said with a smile that covered her pain, "if we're ever around at the same time, we should totally run together."

And so, it was set. For the next few weeks, I had conveniently run into her almost every day. We hit it off so well that we eventually went out to dinner. We'd laughed and joked like two friends who never ran out of things to say. If I had been more emotionally inclined, I would have felt something. Under different circumstances we could have been good friends. But I wasn't who she thought I was, and I was leaving it that way. I continued to put on my facade while we ate at the authentic Italian restaurant she picked out. Everything went great until midway through the conversation. I had only eaten half of my lasagna dinner when out of the blue, she said, "Why are you here, Leslie?"

Staring wide-eyed at my food, the only sound between us was the sound of my fork clanging against the glass plate. No one knew me as Leslie. It was Alex, especially to those involved in my line of work. This just made my job a lot more difficult.

I pretended not to hear her. "Listen, I know why you're here," she sipped her glass of wine as if we were having a normal conversation. While I wanted to sink into my seat, this was not the time. It was the time to get bold and get the upper hand in this conversation. I looked her dead in the face and folded my hands in front of me.

"And what would that reason be?" I said, poker face strong.

"My ex, Raymond, hired you. I know. I'm kind of surprised, though," she said giving her wine glass a swirl before taking another sip, "seeing a woman in this line of work."

You would think this job would get easier...but I don't think it ever does. Some say my gender hinders me, but I've seen some ruthless women that make men look like Ghandi. I'd like to think I was somewhere in the middle. My job didn't make me a saint. In fact, I'm far from it. What I was providing for clients was expensive. It offered peace to one party and permanent heartbreak to another, but ultimately it was more sinful than beneficial.

I was silent but didn't break my stare. She couldn't read it, but she kept talking.

"So how are you going to do it?"

"Do what?" I asked, monotone, no emotion. It was pretty easy to turn it off to keep yourself from being backed into a corner, although I knew exactly what she meant. To try to add a little good deed to my sinful job, I offered a little glimmer of hope for every assignment I took, giving them one last adventure, one last friendship, one last bucket list thing to do. At least when they inevitably died, they would, hopefully, go happily.

"Are we really going to do this dance?"

"Hey, you started it," I leaned back in my seat, arms crossed, and staring her directly in the face. She must be a gambler because she didn't fold at my boldness. I would have thought it was commendable if I wasn't on the receiving end of it.

"I've heard of your work. I've read your resume, seen your portfolio. You're pretty impressive. You were recommended by your friend, Jim, who happens to be my cousin."

"You a cop?" I asked, taking my turn to sip my glass.

"Nope. But I'm making you an offer," she was a totally different person sitting on the other side of this table than she was jogging in the park, but I guess she could say the same about me.

She dropped an envelope on the table.

"I'm sure that's way more than what that cheapskate Raymond offered you. If you do for me what you would have done for him, it's yours."

I reached for the envelope and she grabbed my hand. "I take it we have a deal?"

"You see me reaching for the envelope, don't you?"

She let my hand go and watched me peek into the envelope. From one glance, I could tell it was at least twice as much as Raymond had offered me. We both went back to eating our food until she broke the silence between bites, "So how are you going to do it?"

"I need more information from you before deciding."

I was no longer laughing and chatting with her. Like a robot, I had automatically switched to my professional demeanor.

"Well, let's not talk about that today. Can we just finish our meal like we were and maybe talk about this on the trail tomorrow?" She'd switched back to the Rhonda I met at the park: nice, opening, welcoming, and a hint of hurt and desire for companionship.

I sighed, wanting to say no and call all the shots like usual, but instead I said, "Sure that's fine."
She smiled at me and I smiled back.

"You know, me and you would have made good friends," she said, in the way children do when they meet someone new and ask to be friends.

"It's funny, I was thinking the same thing," I said, involuntarily returning the same enthusiasm.

THE SIGHTS I DIDN'T SEE

When I was about a year old, I finally got the courage to learn how to walk, or so my parents claim. I waddled for a while, fell, and gave up for another month before trying again.

My first real job out of college was not a dream job. Actually, I was a receptionist. "Sorry, he's not in. Can I take a message?" If my salary was based on how many times I said that, my pay would've been at least three times what it actually was.

I took my first drink at 22. Nope, not 21. I thought a "grace period" was necessary. Still don't know what I was thinking.

I learned to ride a bike at age 13, when no one was looking. Come on. 13?

I've wanted to sing all my life. I've given endless shower concerts and multiple "behind the bedroom door" shows to my stuffed animals. Maybe next year. Maybe tomorrow. There are no auditions. I'm not good enough. I'm fine with the job I have now. (I'm not).

And now, as I take this walk, umbrella up to shield my

hair from the rain and I see children jumping in puddles and dancing and riding bikes and embracing the rain, I think...

of all the puddles I never jumped in,

the boys I never kissed,

the time I didn't cut my hair

the vacations I never took by myself

the sights I didn't see

the things I never tried and succeeded as well as the things I never tried and failed.

And the times I never danced in the rain...

A SQUINT FOR A TWINKLE

It's Christmas Eve and I'm sure every kid in America is jittery on sugar cookies that they stole from Santa's plate. They hope to stay awake and catch Santa in the act. Dropping presents. Eating cookies. Feeding reindeer. Anything. They don't know that they'll fall asleep before midnight and will never see him. It's probably for the best. They can stay up for a million years and will never see this so-called Santa Claus. I think that's why God makes the kids fall asleep. It's what's best for them and they don't even know it.

I've been on this earth for thirteen long years and I know the deal about Christmas, but it's up to me to keep the dream alive for my brothers and sisters. It's 12:45 a.m. and I'm about as awake as the noonday rush. I keep trying, but I can't sleep. Slowly, I get up trying not to wake Terry and Stephanie. Terry can't sleep without someone next to her. I walk to the window and check the windowsill for cockroaches. All clear. I pick at the old chipped, white paint and flick away a dead spider.

Refocusing my attention to the sky, I squint to see if I

can see any stars. Living in the city, you never really do. Maybe that's why it's so bad here. We don't have any stars to wish on. My grandma told me they could see all the stars all the time on her farm down in the country. She promised to take us there one day, but you know, people can't always keep their promises. I don't blame her, though. I still believe she would've taken us had she not had that heart attack.

I squint at the midnight sky until my eyes hurt and still nothing. Not even a twinkle.

"Denny, why did you get up?" Terry asked me as she rubbed her eyes. I knew she'd get up without me lying next to her.

"I'm just looking at some stars. Go back to sleep."

"But we don't have stars here. Grandma said so."

Sometimes I feel that Terry is smarter than she should be at six years old.

"You're right. I was just checking."

"Maybe Santa will send you a star for Christmas."

"Yeah, maybe."

I pick away at the paint some more and I can feel Terry staring at me in the dark. She won't go back to sleep unless I come back to bed. I peel a final piece of white paint off, flick it on the floor and join Terry back on the mattress we share, stepping over Stephanie, who would rather have her own space on the floor than share space with anyone on a worn out mattress.

"Denny, do you think we'll have presents for Christmas this year?"

"I promise if you go to sleep right now, you'll have a Christmas surprise tomorrow morning."

Lord, please send a miracle for us tomorrow. For my brothers and sisters. Just send us something to make us happy.

I laid there for another hour, just staring. I tried counting the cracks in the ceiling, but I was robbed of that pleasure by the darkness. Instead, I pictured where I thought they would be. Three long ones in the corners. Twenty-two short ones scattered around. I was in the middle of counting the invisible cracks for the third time when I was interrupted by the door closing downstairs. I gently shake Stephanie awake.

"Steph, sleep next to Terry for a minute."

She shakes her head in obedience and takes my place on the mattress. In this neighborhood, it can be anyone trying to come in the house for any reason. I prepared myself for all the possibilities I could think of, but I hadn't prepared for this one.

"Mom? Is that you?"

In the dark room, I can't just barely tell what she's doing: putting things under our lopsided Christmas tree. She looks up, startled to see me.

"Denny. What are you doing awake?" She says in a half whisper.

"I heard the door. I thought someone was breaking in."

"I told you what to do if there's ever a break-in and I thought I told you to never come exploring to see who it is."

I don't say anything. I didn't have the heart to tell her that

Terry, Stephanie, Bobby, and Johnny needed someone to protect them and it had to be me. She takes a look at my face and even in the dark, she can read it. She comes over and hugs me.

"You should be sleep, baby girl. It's Christmas Eve."

"I know. I couldn't sleep."

She brought her palm to my cheek and says in the sweet way that only the truly caring mothers do, "Go on to bed."

She replaced her palm with a kiss and went to turn on the lights on the tree. It wasn't much to look at, but it made the room look a hundred times better than it did in the dark.

"Ummm..mom?"

"Yea, sweetie?"

"Is it ok if I sleep in your room tonight?"

She looked at me for a moment, then smiled.

"Sure. I'll be up there in a minute."

I barely kept up with my feet as I ran up to her room. Sleeping in her room was rare and for once, I felt like I knew what it was like to be Terry. I waited by the window for my mom to come up the stairs. She didn't have chipped paint on the windowsill like my room did and I could actually see the sky better without all the trees that blocked the view in my room. I gazed at the clear night sky. Squinted. And I know I saw a twinkle.

SKIPPING STONES

~~~

I marched out of my dad's lake cabin and began on the familiar dirt trail along the trees. I'd purposely picked a fight with Dad to get an excuse to have some time alone. This was our seventh year coming to this cabin. We came every year the second weekend in May and I was old enough to know why he chose this weekend to come. Now that I was 17, I knew that this would probably be our last annual cabin trip and I didn't know how to feel about it.

I walked the trail and knew I had been rude the entire trip. We had been at the cabin for two days and only had a day and a half left. I walked until I couldn't see the cabin anymore and sat on a tree stump, facing the water. I picked up a few rocks and started throwing them into the water. Mom used to love skipping stones. I never actually learned how to do it. I remembered the words she used to tell me when she tried to teach me how to do it.

"Ok, honey, get a flat rock. It has to be flat. Don't throw it like a jump shot in basketball. Throw it like you're throwing a

CD at someone you hate. Like that Cindy girl you were telling me about."

We would laugh and I would throw the stone into the lake. It never quite skipped and she would say, "It's ok, it just takes practice." After a few tries, I got frustrated and threw the rocks on the ground. "Forget it," I'd say and walk away.

That was seven years ago.

I tried to skip another one. I stood up, took the flat stone, and threw it, just like I was throwing a CD. Not one skip. It just sank.

"Whatever," I said out loud and sat back down on the stump.

I knew my dad meant well, but I didn't want to be here anymore. It didn't feel right to be here without Mom. Each year it felt like more and more memories of her were fading away and although I was happy with escaping the pain of having her gone the last few years, this year I just wanted to remember her rather than try and get my mind off her. I sat on the stump, staring at the water, and replayed the last conversation I'd had with her, one of the only things I remember so vividly.

∽

"Mom, can you take me to the park? I told Madison I'd meet her there."

"No, Jordan. I have to go to the church for a meeting. Ask

your dad."

"I did. He told me to ask you," I said as I went to the re-frigerator and grabbed a Gatorade.

"Can't you walk to the park?" she asked as she left to the living room in a hurry. I followed.

"It's six blocks!" I said getting a little annoyed.

"You've walked six blocks before, Jordan." I could tell she was getting equally annoyed.

"But I have to take my basketball. We're practicing for the game tomorrow."

"And you can't walk with a basketball in your hand?"

"Moooom," I whined.

"Jordan, stop. You're getting too old for this...why can't your dad take you?"

"He has the seminar to speak at tonight."

"Oh, right I forgot."

She sat there thinking for a minute and went back to flip-ping the couch cushions over.

"Ok, I'll take you because I don't want you leaving with no one here. Help me find my keys. I'm already late to the meet-ing."

"Got em," I said as I got them out of the kitchen drawer.

∾

She dropped me off at the park and promised to pick me

up after her meeting. She never did. Madison's mother had to take me to her house and my dad picked me up from there and broke the news that my mom had gotten into an accident after dropping me off.

I threw a huge stone into the water, more so out of anger than trying to skip it.

"Whoa, you almost had the fish jumping out of the water with that one," my dad's voice came after the splash of the rock.

"Dad come on. Don't sneak up on me like that," I said without taking my eyes off the water. He sighed and stood next to me, looking at the water like I did. After a few moments of silence, he said, "You know your mom and I bought this cabin about fifteen years ago?"

"Really?"

"Yeah. We sometimes came here while you were at camp to do some fishing."

"I didn't know Mom liked to fish."

"She didn't, but you know how much she liked the lake and just being outdoors connecting with nature."

"Yeah," was all I said.

"Jordie if you want to cut our trip short, we can go home. I don't want to force you to stay here."

I felt like a real jerk when he said that. I knew he was trying to make me feel comfortable just like he's done every day for the last seven years. And now that I knew he spent time with Mom at this cabin, I realized, for the first time, that it wasn't that he was handling Mom's death so well, but that he was hiding his pain from me.

"No, Dad, we can stay. I just...I miss her, you know."

"Yeah, I know," he said in almost a whisper.

"Sometimes I think if I hadn't asked Mom to take me to the park that day, maybe the accident wouldn't have happened." He placed his hand on my shoulder and I tried hard not to cry.

"Don't ever think that way. It's not your fault."

I stood up and buried my head in his chest and he hugged me back. We stayed that way for a few minutes and I knew he would hold me as long as I needed it.

"You know, if I hadn't been so preoccupied with my seminar...I could've taken you that day."

I stared up at him, not letting him go.

"Dad, that wasn't your fault."

"I know. It took me a few years to realize I had to stop blaming myself. I don't want you carrying that guilt either."

"I know..." I laid my head on his chest again.

"If you ever want to talk about it, you know I'll listen. I don't want you to think you have to go off on your own."

"I know, Dad. I was just trying to skip a stone like Mom used to do."

He let me go and looked at me.

"Let me see you try."

"No, I suck."

He laughed and picked one up himself. He threw it up in

the air a few times and caught it. Then he threw it in the water like Mom used to do and it skipped.

"I didn't know you knew how to skip them too," I said.

"Of course. I was the one who showed your mother."

I picked one up and threw it in like I did earlier.

"Well no wonder it's not skipping. You're throwing it a little too close. Throw it a little harder and further. Flick it instead of tossing it."

He showed me by example.

"Mom told me to throw it like a CD, like I'm mad at someone."

He laughed and I laughed too.

"Well, I'm not surprised. She wasn't the best at teaching."

I smiled. We spent the next few hours sitting by the lake talking about our memories of Mom. Dad told me things I'd never even known about her. I reminisced all the things I could remember. By the time sunset hit, we were still talking and laughing and ready to call it a night. We stood up to head back to the cabin and I picked up another stone and did as my dad said earlier. I relaxed, threw it a little harder, further, let it glide. And it skipped twice.

SEEING RED

He saw her only twice. Once when he passed her on the street and once on the news.

He didn't even know why he remembered her, but he did. Maybe it was the deep, perfectly red hair. Maybe it was the piercing in her nose. Maybe it was the way she shot a glance at him when he stared at the scar right above her left eye. Either way, he recognized her.

"...*took in excess of $10,000 after shooting two police officers. One dead, the other in critical condition. Police are still on the lookout for...*"

He looked at her picture. She didn't look like a criminal. She looked...unhuman. Her eyes looked past the camera. It was an old mugshot. He knew it because the deep red in her hair was a midnight blue. It didn't appeal to him as much. The red was intriguing. It reminded him of...life, death...a past version of himself. It aroused him in ways he wasn't ready for. Not necessarily sexually, but mentally and emotionally.

"...*last seen in Borrough County. Police lost her in the*

chase and are now sending helicopters on the way..."

He was titillated by the whole thing way more than he should have been. And the woman...God, he missed her name. There was something so captivating about her that only he could see. Others would have thought she was crazy, but he saw through the surface.

They showed a snapshot of her in the bank, gun drawn at the officer and something in him leapt. It was drawing him in more and more with each second. He went into his bedroom, grabbed the lockbox, and put the combination in. He grabbed his old Glock out the box. It was new when he bought it and it was still in great shape. He didn't know what he was doing. Or why he was doing it. At this point, he was just moving on instinct. Pure flesh. His mind was out of the question. He went back to the living room, grabbed his keys, and headed north. He didn't know exactly where he was going. He just knew he was headed towards Borrough County.

MAILMAN KNOWLEDGE

~~~

8838: Ms. Jones was a single woman. She didn't like other people, but you could tell she was nice. She got newsletters from children's charities, so I figured she'd given a lot of money to them. She didn't have her own children, so she sponsored other kids. She was never at the door when I delivered her stuff. I think she liked being alone...or told herself she did.

8801: The Morleys weren't a particularly close family. I saw them coming out of their house once. Three kids and a fourth on the way. The kids were screaming the way out of control children do. But the mom, Joyce Morley, had a spending problem. I delivered packages from expensive boutiques to her all the time, which was usually accompanied by a letter for her husband from a collection agency.

8812: Bradley Callahan was a young guy, who had women coming in and out all the time. This is a fact, not a judgment. At least once a week, when I would drop off his mail in the morning, there was a different woman each time coming out the house. He loved all kinds of women. Each one looking incredibly different than the last. He didn't get any mail, really, though. Except Playboy and Architectural Digest Magazines.

8820: Angela Bogart...Angela Bogart was someone I always hoped I would meet. She liked books. She ordered them all the time. She, like Ms. Jones, gave to charities. But she also liked to work out. She subscribed to fitness magazines. She got a lot of handwritten letters and cards, especially around the holidays, more than anyone else I ever delivered for, so I figured a lot of people liked her. She lived alone because all the mail for the address was only delivered to her. I didn't see strange people coming in and out. In fact, I never saw her coming out. Until last Thursday. I walked up the steps to place her mail in her box. A magazine, a bill, and junk mail. And that's when I saw her walk out the house. She had on black and green yoga pants with a matching neon green tank top. I assumed she was either going to the gym or going jogging.

"Hi," I said with an awkward smile.

"Hi," she said and proceeded to lock her door.

I looked at her. She turned back to me and I froze, realizing I had on my dorky beige shorts and pale blue shirt like I'm going on a safari. Whose idea was it to make us mailmen wear stupid stuff like this? Could it be any more of a woman repellant? I handed her mail out to her, gesturing to her, asking whether she wanted to take it or if she wanted me to put it in the mailbox.

"Oh, I'll take it," she said.

I stood there for an extra few seconds until I realized she

was waiting for me to leave and I was being creepy.

"Going jogging?" I asked trying to strike up conversation.

"Yep."

"Cool. I like to jog too."

"It's great for the body," she said without looking at me, looking through her mail.

I could tell she was barely listening and half interested.

"Well, have a nice day," I said and started walking down the stairs.

"Yeah, you too."

I headed down the block to the next house.

"Hey, wait!" she said. I turned around a little too eagerly.

"You looking for a jogging partner?" she asked.

"Yeah actually I would like one."

"Hmm...maybe we could go jogging one day if you don't mind."

"No...no, not at all."

"Cool. I'll see you around."

She took off jogging down the block and around the corner. I was excited for a minute, until I couldn't remember the last time I'd actually jogged.

PEACE IN THE RAIN

When it rains in Somerston, everyone takes cover, because we always knew there was a probability of a tornado. I hated it and I couldn't wait to leave Somerston as soon as I could. My best friend, Haley, on the other hand, loved it. I still remember the first time I'd seen a tornado hit us. It devastated our town so much. Grocery stores were closed. We had no electricity for days. Cars and patio furniture ended up on the other end of the neighborhood. But, honestly, it was the least of everyone's problems, because we were all dealing with some type of other grief on our own. Mine, I believe, was more than a 13-year-old girl should have to go through.

It was a Wednesday at exactly 1:12pm. I remember looking at my watch when the sirens began, followed by our vice principal getting on the PA System with her professional, yet phony authoritative voice, "Teachers. Staff. And students. A tornado warning has been issued for this county. This is not a drill-" No one heard what she said next. The lights went out, a sign that the storm had just knocked out the electricity, and with that, the classroom went into a frenzy:

"Oh my God, oh my God, oh my God."

"Where's my boyfriend?"

"I have to call my mom."

The rest was filled with hysteria. People crying, some pacing, others grabbing friends. And one-third of the class ran out the door. Poor Ms. Kim couldn't even gain control of the class. She was only 5'1" and spoke softly so any effort to calm us went unheard. I, contrary to most others, was eerily stoic. I didn't know what to do. I didn't know if I should be nervous. Or afraid. I literally froze and watched as everything happened around me, although I felt like I wasn't really there.

Somerston was such a hick town and we got tornadoes often. There was nothing worth seeing except the Somerston High School football games and a few local fairs. The rest was corn field. Perfect tornado scenery, but even though we had heard of them and had scares, most of us students had never seen or experienced one. They usually hit the farms and died before hitting the town. The last one that hit was nine years ago, when most of us were too young to remember, and even if we did remember, we were most likely in the comforts of our parents.

We had a tornado drill at least once a year to prepare ourselves for this exact situation and evidently, it was all for nothing. I finally stood up out of my seat and walked into the hallway.

"Come back here! Do not go in that hallway!"

Ms. Kim called to me, but as I listened to her, I couldn't

actually hear her. It was like the words were traveling to my ears, but not communicating with my brain. All I heard was the rumbling thunder outside and the downpour hitting the gutters of the building. I felt like a zombie. Although I could walk, and wanted to stop, I couldn't. My legs were heavy as I walked probably as slow as I ever walked in my life, but I couldn't stop them from moving.

I stood in the doorway and watched the hysteria. Some students had actually followed instructions and kneeled, by the lockers, facing the wall, with their hands folded behind their necks, but with the mayhem of everyone else running around and the teachers running after them, it actually made them look like the idiots.

I scanned the hallway and was immediately snapped out of my daze when I saw Haley, who also had a zombie-like look on her face as she robotically marched down the hallway.

"Haley!" I ran to her and pulled her in a hug.

"Oh my God, Riley!"

We stood there hugging for a few seconds until she broke it.

"Isn't this cool?"

"I wouldn't exactly call this cool."

"I mean, everyone is so scared of the tornado. It probably won't even come. I mean, we get tornado scares all the time."

"Yeah, I guess. Still, I think we need to take cover somewhere."

She looked around, searching for a safe space.

"Yeah, not up here, though…hey! I'm sure my friend Jackson can let us in the A/V room."

"Good thinking!"

The A/V room was in the basement and had no windows. It was probably the safest place for us to be. We sped down the hallway, quietly so not to draw attention to ourselves.

"You know, I just want to see it."

"See what?" I asked.

"See the tornado. The rain. Everything."

I shrugged in response.

"Hey, let's look out the window real quick. Just a peak."

"I don't know, Hales."

"Fine. You big baby. I'll look. I find peace in the rain."

I stood in the corner of the main hallway as Haley made her way towards the front door. The windows to the front door were too high, so she grabbed a chair and stood on top of it. As soon as she peaked her head into it, it shattered, and I saw my best friend get thrown by some unknown force all the way down the hallway. It was so powerful, that it knocked me back a few feet and I hit the ground, not before banging my head on a locker.

"HALEY!" I never screamed so loud in my life.

I stood to my feet, ready to run after her, but collapsed in my efforts. I tried as best as I could to get to her, but it was to no avail. Head spinning, all I heard was more shattering accompanied with heart-wrenching yelling. It was as if everyone was screaming out to God, begging Him to stop this. A second later, my legs gave way and the room grew dark. And when I finally woke back up a few hours later in a hospital bed, I knew that I would be facing my upcoming high school days alone. Living them out for both me and Haley.

QUARTER IN THE FOUNTAIN

He stood at the fountain, watching the water cascade down the concrete ducklings. Blazer casually thrown over his shoulder, he flipped the quarter into the air and watched it make a bubble in the water. His mom had given it to him. She'd hoped it would reconcile their relationship. Although the coin itself had no value to anyone else, to him it did. He hadn't had anything else from any other travel excursions with her. In fact, he really didn't have anything to remind him of her…and he never did.

It wasn't fair.

Why after all these years must she actually give him something to remember? Why did they have to take that stupid trip? Was it really better to experience some form of love and lose it than to not have it at all? He didn't think so.

He thought about calling her for the hundredth time, but he knew the only thing that would result in was him binge watching Netflix and ordering pizza to forget he even tried.

"Her phone is probably just turned off," he thought to himself. And with that he smiled. Because he knew she had some financial troubles and that was a perfectly logical explanation. He pulled out his phone, called her one more time. When it went to voicemail, he left a message.

"Hey Lisa..err Mom..it's me again! I don't know if your phone is turned off, but I was just calling to see how you were doing. I was thinking of our trip to Canada. We should take another trip together don't you think?"

He paused as if waiting for a response.

"Anyway, call me back!…Oh, umm..I love you."

He reached into the fountain and grabbed the coin. Disregarding his soaked work shirt, he looked at the moose on the coin, reading the word "Canada" on it. He'd studied it so much that he knew where each and every bump was on both the front and back of it. He tucked it in his pocket and began to walk to his car, checking his phone on the way.

A BRIEF ESCAPE

~~~

"I was just kind of hoping you'd, y'know…fall in love with me."

She paused for a second, then continued tending to his wound, focusing her attention to the cut above his eye rather than looking into his eyes.

"What do you mean?" She continued to clean blood that wasn't there. He grabbed her hand to stop her from cleaning his face.

"You know what I mean."

He forced her to look at him. It was the only way he ever had even a glimpse to know what was in her head.

She looked away, at the tile, at the towel hanging on the rack, at the floor, anything other than him. He grabbed her chin with gentle authority and forced her to face him.

"Don't do that," he said.

She looked him square in the eyes for the first time and she saw the pain that he was trying to hide. It wasn't that she didn't love him. She didn't want to go into this merry go round with him…again.

"Eli-"

It was the first time she'd called him Eli in about a year and she knew he picked up on it by the way he perked up.

"I know you love me," he interrupted her.

She dropped the towel she was holding, wiggled out of his grip, and walked over to the bedroom. She knew he'd follow her, but she needed a few seconds to think. Suddenly, the apartment was feeling much smaller than it was.

She canvased the familiar bedroom and wanted to cry. Eli was always taking hits for her and for everyone else, literally and figuratively. She appreciated it, but she knew what it all meant. It wasn't clean love. It wasn't romantic love. It wasn't the kind of love you see on tv. It was premature love. Even after two years of the back and forth, she knew he wasn't ready for it and she couldn't feed into it. She couldn't allow him to keep taking hits… and she couldn't allow herself to be in that vulnerable position of receiving that phone call that he'd been beat or shot and killed and her world coming crashing down.

Like clockwork, he followed her into the bedroom. "You never tell me what you're thinking," he said as a half statement, half question.

"I told you we're just friends Eli. Why can't you accept that?"

He grabbed her hand and instead of arguing with her like he usually did, he pressed his lips to hers. This was unlike him. It took her by surprise. She was so thrown off by the surprise that she didn't think about pulling away. She froze and for the first few seconds, the kiss was one of the most awkward ones they both had experienced. It was rushed, unprepared, and unsynchronized, but in a split second, it changed. He grabbed her waist and slowed down, waiting for her to catch up.

And she did.

She wrapped her delicate arms around his broad shoulders and gave in and kept kissing him. She didn't want to break the kiss because she didn't know where they would stand after this…and she wasn't ready to know.

COFFEE AND PINES

The morning rush was the worst. Everyone standing elbow to elbow in that crowded little cafe. In his town, it almost put Starbucks to shame. Simply called The Caf, the place sucked you in with the aroma of caffeine as soon as you hit the door. The smell was softened a bit accompanied with the scent of fresh bagels and cinnamon scones. But, he didn't like that. He preferred the smell of the pines The Caf brought at night, when everyone was cleaning and closing, and the only thing left was the scent from the pine trees that surrounded the back of the cafe.

So he went to The Caf at night. The coffee was never good that late, but he drank it anyway. For him, it was the best alternative to alcohol, and it kept him awake to create the illusion that he was working on his laptop. He ordered his usual: just a regular coffee. Black. And took his usual table by the window. It was a little chilly, especially at this time of year, but he needed the view. He needed to see the pine trees he was smelling, even though he could never work his way up to go near them. He just admired them from a distance. And for now, that was enough.

As he waited for his coffee, he opened his laptop and began absentmindedly scrolling through emails. Most of them were work related. Clients and potential clients all wanting something from him. Requests ranging from people wanting him to design a book cover, fix a billboard typo, or change a website design and he scrolled past them all. He didn't feel like being pulled on. In fact, he wasn't in the mood to work at all, even though he worked better at night to keep his mind off things, but that wasn't the case that night. He was ready to close his laptop and just pull out a book instead, when an email caught his eye. It was from Ana.

Why would Ana be emailing me? Does she even know how to email? He opened it, nervously. The last time he spoke with Ana was in a courtroom and it was not a good conversation. She'd said everything her daughter wanted to say and more. He closed his eyes and prepared himself for what it could read. Was he being served again? Do they do that through email nowadays? The momentary suspense outweighed his fear and he began to read: *"Henry, I know it has been a long time and I know I could get into trouble with contacting you, but I wanted to reach out anyway. I hope all is well with you. I'm hoping during this holiday you can find joy. Consider the photo below my Christmas gift to you. Please don't let my daughter know I sent this to you. Little Hen misses you, although he doesn't want to be called that anymore now that he's 11. We call him Henry now. Take care."*

He opened the attachment and saw his "Little Hen", the spitting image of himself at that age, smiling too big and too close to the camera in his full winter gear. It had been four years and he didn't how to feel about the photo. He froze staring at it until the barista set his black coffee on the table. He took a sip and looked out the window. Then he drank the rest of the coffee in one long gulp. It was way too hot and way too strong, but he forced it down because he secretly just wanted the sting it gave his throat. It was all he had. That and The Caf. They both gave him what he needed, but oddly couldn't have.

He looked at the photo again and instead of looking at the boy's face, he looked around it. Snow everywhere. They both loved snow. They both loved this season, holidays and all. And behind the boy was a row of pine trees. He tried to imagine being there, so he took a big inhale in the cafe soaking in every bit of the scent he could, closing his eyes, wishing he was in that snow. And as he exhaled, he released both his breath and his tears.

BURNED BRIDGES

Aaron sat in the uncomfortable terminal chair with his feet propped up on his suitcase. He'd been watching planes take off and land for the last three hours. He was too tired to move and too nervous to eat anything. So he stayed glued to his seat, just waiting and watching. With each passing minute, he got closer to seeing Bryan, someone who until eight years ago, he'd shared ghost stories with at sleepovers, cannon balled with into the swimming pool, and gotten scars with from popping too many wheelies on their bikes. He didn't think Bryan was having any sleepovers now and he definitely wasn't diving into pools or popping any wheelies. Aaron was to blame for that...at least that's what he'd told himself every week since the last time they saw each other. Now they were both of legal adult age and he didn't know what to expect. Maybe he shouldn't have answered his email about meeting together in their hometown. It'd been eight years and he wasn't even sure if he would be meeting the same person.

∾

"They're just glasses, Bry. No one is going to care," ten-year-old Aaron tried to console his best friend. As they both got older, Aaron began to draw the attention of fifth grade girls while Bryan started to struggle with poor teeth and poor eyesight, both of which required corrective measures that, in the fifth grade, was a big deal.

"Easy for you to say," he pouted.

They sat by the pool in Aaron's parents' backyard, feet dangling in the water. It was the only place that Bryan's mother was comfortable with him going alone. Bryan's father left when he was four and his mother didn't have any other children. She was past child rearing age when she had Bryan and saw him as her one and only jewel in the world. And she would do anything to protect that jewel no matter how ridiculous anyone else thought it was.

"You want to go swimming?" he asked trying to cheer him up. Bryan shook his head no.

Aaron jumped up. He knew this would take drastic measures.

"I saw this move on wrestling yesterday. Let me show you!"

"I don't wanna."

"Aw come on. You afraid I'm gonna kick your butt?"

This worked. A slight smile crossed Bryan's face and he slowly stood up. Their version of wrestling was a mixture of "tag" coupled with kicking and punching the air.

They ran around the lawn while Aaron's dad did some yard work, screaming and kicking and punching without a care in the world. It was a normal day until they'd reached the fire pit. Aaron wasn't paying attention and tripped over one of the chairs, crashing into Bryan and causing him to fall backwards into the pit. His subsequent screams could be heard from a mile away. Aaron had never seen Bryan flail around like he did trying to get the fire off him. In the hysteria, Bryan then tripped over the same chair that Aaron did and fell onto the pavement. Aaron was frozen in panic and shock. He was moved out the way by his dad who had ran to the rescue and was trying to put the fire out his son's best friend using a towel that was in the yard.

"Son! Go call 911!"

Aaron stood staring at Bryan.

"Aaron, NOW!"

Aaron sat in the waiting room that day sandwiched between his mother and father. He was in such a daze, he didn't think of what Bryan's poor mother would think. She came storming through the waiting room doors, in full hysteria mode.

"Where is my son?! WHERE IS MY SON?!"

Aaron's dad stood up and grabbed her arm to try and calm her down.

"Don't touch me!"

Her gaze turned to Aaron, "You!! This is your fault. You killed my son!"

Aaron's dad stood in front of his son to block her from

getting any closer, while his more confrontational mother stood up and raised her voice, pointing her finger at her face, "Now you just wait a minute!"

They began to argue and exchange a few expletives, both insulting the other's parenting until Aaron's dad spoke up, "Hey! Stop it! It's alright Ms. Bates, we're leaving." At that, his dad hurried his wife and son out the door. It would be a week until Bryan was able to come home and another week before Aaron could work up the courage to go over his house to check on him. After the episode in the hospital, he didn't want to ask his parents to go. He just went on his way home from school. He knocked on the door and a tired looking Ms. Bates answered, "You have some nerve coming here," she said in a quiet, eery voice. Her eyes looked like she had slept a total of eight hours in the past two weeks.

"Hi Ms. Bates...umm...is Bryan ok?"

"What do you think?" she folded her arms and waited for his answer.

"Sorry. Can I see him? I just came to check on him."

"You'll do no such thing. He's sleeping now anyway." Aaron paused for a minute to swallow the lump that was forming in his throat.

"I'm really sorry, Ms. Bates. I didn't mean to-"

"There's a reason I didn't let Bryan go anywhere even when everyone was telling me I was crazy. Then you came along, and he had a friend and I figured, sure why not. Then this happens...I trusted you."

The tears were falling down Aaron's face at this point, but Ms. Bates continued as if she didn't notice, "The doctors say he'll be lucky if he can walk again, among other things."

"I'm really sorry. I didn't mean to. I just-"

"Please don't come over here again."

With that, Ms. Bates shut the door and Aaron was left staring at the door alone. After that he just ran. He ran the entire three blocks to his home.

~

Aaron checked his watch. 3:27pm. It was time for Bryan's flight to arrive. He looked out the window and, right on time, he watched it pull in. He could hear his heart beating in his ears and it was like he was ten years old again. He stood up and kept his distance, but his eyes never left the gate. After ten minutes of anticipation, he perked up at the sight: a young lanky 18-year-old guy, who looked like he could be Bryan's older brother. He still wore glasses, but the braces were gone. He was in a wheelchair being escorted by one of the flight attendants. Aaron's heart sank as the guilt began to slowly creep back into him. His eyes never left Bryan as he approached, and he began to notice other little physical intricacies. He had facial hair now. He noticed some slight skin disfiguration in his neck, but other than that, no serious visible burns. In fact, he didn't look like the shy kid who was afraid to wear his glasses. He actually had a strange aura of confidence as he flirted with the young flight attendant assisting him into the airport.

Aaron walked toward him, and Bryan looked at him with a smile. Bryan looked at the flight attendant, "Alright, this is my stop, honey. But you should still call me sometime." She giggled and left the two of them together.

"Bryan! Hi!" Aaron stood frozen not sure if he should hug him or not.

"You gonna hug me or what? Or are you going to try another wrestling move on me?"

Aaron looked at him blankly until Bryan looked at him with a smile and laughed. Aaron returned the smile and bent down to hug his friend.

IMMORTAL DATE

The thunder woke me and I absentmindedly turned in my bed to reach for her. But she wasn't there. Anastasia to most, only Ana to me. She hated it when other people called her Ana. That was something that was only reserved for me and I can't say I didn't like it. She was the bravest woman I had known, yet something about thunderstorms terrified her entire being. I'd wake up and watch her shivering, arms wrapped around her own waist in bed, trying to calm herself. She didn't want me to know how much it scared her. I never talked about it or asked her about it. I just turned over every night it happened and wrapped my arms around her. She would stop shivering, warm up a bit, and fall right back to sleep. I selfishly loved these moments. They were the times I felt I could protect her the most.

She was the only wife I didn't divorce. She was the ninth. It wasn't that I didn't love any of them. Just keeping up with the aging process proved nearly impossible during those times, but I made an exception for Ana. The 1960s didn't have as many resources as we do now, but I made it work. Finding ways to gray my hair was easy. Aging my skin was the hard part, but as her eyesight worsened, it worked to my advantage. After a while, I just wore long sleeves and she barely noticed the difference.

We went from hearing, "They're such a cute couple" to "Is that her son?" to "What a nice grandson." Her memory served as a great cover for my condition, because after a while, she didn't know if I was her grandson or her husband. Most often, I was a stranger. I guess it worked out for my identity, but it didn't work out for me. It was the first time I felt what "til death do us part" meant and I knew that meant her death and not mine. It was the first time I stuck it out until the end, and I wanted it to be the last time. Even now, almost 50 years later, I still think about her. Here I was, my physical appearance frozen somewhere around 26, laying in the bedroom of my apartment that I shared with my roommate, dragging to get out of bed at noon.

I made my way to the couch where my roommate, Lex, was sitting, eating a peanut butter sandwich as a break between film classes, black rock t-shirt matching her fingernails and she had the attitude to complete the ensemble.

"You been in that bed all day, dude?"

"Yeah," I said making my way to the refrigerator to drink orange juice out of the carton.

"You really need to go get a job or something. You asked your parents for money or something yet?"

"Hey! I'm paying rent, aren't I? That's all that matters."

I loved Lex. She had become like a sister to me in the last

two years. She looked out for me almost too much.

"So, I met this girl today."

"Lex--"

"Hear me out! She's really nice. She's new to town and she's looking for someone to show her around."

"Why can't you do it?"

"Well, I figured you've been living here longer than I have that you could show her. Plus, Jo, I think it would be great to finally get out and meet someone. As long as we've known each other and been living together, I've never seen you with a woman."

I sighed. I didn't know what to say. I'd never told anyone about my condition, and I didn't think I wanted to start now.

"Listen, would it be easier if we made it a double? I'll go with you and bring someone."

I didn't want to date again. I didn't want to go through the inevitable separation and heartbreak that I'd most likely have to be the one to deal with. But there was more I didn't want. I didn't want to mourn Ana anymore. I didn't want to remember how she looked or smelled. I didn't want to roll over during anymore thunderstorms. And there was no way I'd be able to escape the separation when those around me passed away and I stayed here because I would go through a similar heartbreak when I would have to say goodbye to Lex and anyone else I crossed paths with. And although I didn't want to go through the goodbyes, I didn't want to miss out on everything that came after the hellos.

"So, what do you think?" she asked.

I sighed again. "Fine. What do you have in mind?"

MASTERPIECE

"Who were you?" he whispered, staring at the wonderful masterpiece that graced the wall. Jim would be retiring in about 30 days and he looked good for it. That's what working on the force did to you. The physical exertion either prolonged your youth or accelerated your age. Lucky for Jim, he was able to benefit from the former. He loved his job as a detective. It was bittersweet being able to retire. He'd be able to finally spend time with Margaret and she'd never have to worry if he would be killed on the job. However, as happy as he was, there was a bit of him that was a little unhappy. Of all the cases he worked, there was one that meant the most to him and he never solved it: The Disappearance of Paolo Marino.

Unfortunately, the man had disappeared two years after Jim was born so information was limited, but he used all his connections to try and figure out what happened to him to give him some kind of peace. It was a situation that had been close to Jim's heart ever since he first became detective, but after inquiring about it when he was a rookie, he eventually blew it off just like everyone else did. Now, he had to have the answers. Chances are Paolo was dead, but that didn't stop Jim from wanting to know of his life and how it may have ended.

Leslie, the mother of Paolo's only child, had told Jim most of what he knew about him. Jim remembered the days following her around in the kitchen when he was just a young boy. Leslie worked at The Old Thyme Market, where locals would stop in to grab their groceries and travelers would make a pit stop to grab a burger. Leslie worked in the kitchen, preparing produce as gifts for travelers. Jim enjoyed helping her snap peas and bag peanuts, but mostly, he came to be with Leslie and sneak in some good food.

"Mom, tell me about Paolo!"

That's Paolo the Great to you!" she'd say. She would stop snapping peas and ruffle his hair.

"Paolo the Great!" he'd say emphatically, pointing his finger to the sky.

"Well...Paolo was a miiiiighty explorer from Italy. He was a warrior! But he was also gentle and kind, just like you."

That part always made Jim smile.

"Tell me more, Mama!"

"Well, Paolo was a man of the people. When his family was in trouble, he left Italy to find a new place for them to be safe and have a better life. He went faaaaar and wide," she illustrated her point by raising the palm of her hand and letting it scan the air as she looked off into the distance, "And do you know where he landed?"

"In America!"

"That's right, sonny. And do you know what he did when he came to America?"

"Tell me!" Jim said emphatically.

"He couldn't bring his family right away, but he found some land and bought it. He built houses and a library and stores...even the one you're standing in right now!"

Jim gasped in delight.

"He also made sure all the children were taken care of and went to a good school. But there was one baby he loved the most-"

Jim cut her off to finish the story with his favorite part, "That's me!"

He stood on top of a basket and stuck out his chest.

"That's right, baby boy."

"And that's why we have the same last name! Because he wants me to be just like him!"

"You got it!" Leslie said, picking the boy up from the basket and giving him an embrace and a kiss.

"Mommy, do you think Paolo will come back to find me?" Jim asked.

"I hope so, son. Paolo has a lot to do, but guess what? He left something for you!"

Jim gasped, getting excited again, "Oh my gosh! What is it?"

"Close your eyes! And no peeking."

He covered his eyes in anticipation.

"Open your hand," she instructed.

He opened them and kept his eyes closed. She placed a golden pocket watch in his hand. He opened his eyes and you'd swear it was Christmas morning.

"Don't lose it, sonny! And if Paolo comes back, you can show him that you kept it."

It was one of the few times Jim was speechless. He took the watch and put it in his pocket. He didn't say anything. Instead he hugged his mom tightly and went back to snapping peas.

As Jim grew older, he began to realize the story was a bit more than a fabrication. Jim held onto the story and the pocket watch until he'd become a detective some thirty years ago. He was finally able to get the information his mother refused to disclose, and the story was far from Paolo being an explorer. After some searching while working through his lunch break one day, Jim discovered that Paolo was nothing more than a criminal immigrant from Italy who'd gotten deported. And the crime? Murder. Jim fought the idea for a while. Maybe it was a misunderstanding. Maybe it was a case of mistaken identity. But after badgering his mother, she'd finally disclosed the truth. It was more than Jim wanted to take so he shoved the pocket watch into his attic along with his idea of Paolo Marino. It wasn't until he was facing retirement that he realized he still wanted the closure to know why this stranger had done what he did and abandoned his only son.

He'd convinced himself for thirty years that it didn't matter, but it did. And Jim could get as old as he wanted, but he could never outgrow his thoughts.

After doing another search like he'd done when he first began his career, he found three addresses associated with Paolo. The first two were dead ends. The third was the one he was standing in right now: an abandoned old beach house. There wasn't much inside except an old dusty couch and a television set that looked like the first tv ever made. But the thing that stood out from everything else was a large painting on the wall. It was kept in a glass case for protection.

At first, Jim couldn't imagine why Paolo would keep a random piece of art on the wall until he saw "P. Marino" scribbled in the bottom corner in silver ink. That's when he took a closer look. At first glance, it looked like a mural of different things happening to different people at once, but a closer look revealed that the artist had painted the same person in different scenes. The first was of a thin man with thick black hair on a boat docked in the United States. The next was of a man at a store that looked just like the Old Thyme. The man was accompanied by a young-curly haired woman, resembling Leslie. There were others with the man and friends and other people Jim didn't recognize, but the one that stood out the most was one with the man holding a baby. In this scene, he'd painted the date on the man's shirt, Jim's birthday. Jim ran his fingers over the glass in front of the baby in the painting. "My gosh," he whispered.

He stared at it for a few minutes until a spot of red in the corner of the work of art caught his eye. There was a masked man standing over another man, gun in hand. The thick-haired skinny man stood over the body, next to the masked gunman with tears coming down his face. It was the darkest part of the whole painting, but the most graphic. He took a step back in shock and took everything in as a whole. It was beautiful and confusing and depressing and hopeful all at the same time. He immediately removed the painting from the glass and rolled it up to take home with him. But before he finished packing it away, he noticed an address on the back. He didn't recognize it. It was an Italian address. He stared at it for a moment before finally letting the tears form in his eyes.

"I'm sorry, Dad." He didn't know what he was apologizing for. Maybe for hating him all these years. Maybe for having the power to clear his name and never doing anything about it. Maybe for believing the worst about him instead of giving the benefit of the doubt. He wasn't sure. He wasn't even sure what the painting all meant. But maybe he could change all that. After all, he was retiring so he'd have time on his hands. Maybe he and Margaret could fix up the beach house. They hadn't gone on a vacation in years. Maybe they could go to Italy. He tucked the painting underneath his arm, wiped the tears from his face, and headed to his car, a smile on his face as he thought of the new adventure he'd begin in 30 days.

MS. DARLENE

～～～

Ms. Darlene Vida lived across the street and three houses down. People who knew her called her Ms. Darlene. She insisted on it over Ms. Vida, for whatever reason. Younger children would ask, "Ms. Vida, do you need help with your groceries?"

She waved them off, politely of course. "No, honey. But call me Ms. Darlene."

She lived at 2135 South Lake for as long as she lived. She never moved; exposing her life to multiple generations who had come and gone out the neighborhood.

The first time I saw Ms. Darlene was my first summer in the neighborhood. My friends and I were playing jump rope. It was the beginning of June and we were pretty ecstatic to be out of school. All of the neighborhood kids came out to play as an unofficial enjoyment kind of thing. Ms. Darlene had a dog then. My mom said it was to keep her company, which I didn't understand at the time because she had a husband.

"She needs a different kind of company," was all my mom said and we never really spoke about it after that.

She called the dog Darwin, and so everyone else did. Darwin had ran out the house per usual, because he was a playful kind of dog always barking and jumping when he saw people, especially kids, probably because Ms. Darlene didn't have any of her own. Darwin ran to us and tripped over our jump rope, completely interrupting our "All in together, any kind of weather…" All the girls loved him and didn't mind the intrusion as we each petted him and he stood there in childish arrogance, tongue sticking out, basking in our affections. Ms. Darlene ran outside to find Darwin, right before her husband, whose last name I'm sure wasn't Vida, came outside and started shouting a few obscene things to the dog and one or two not much nicer words to Ms. Darlene.

I picked up Darwin before he had the chance to start racing down the block again.

"It's ok, Mr. Vida. We don't mind Darwin being outside," I said trying to keep the moment as calm as possible.

"My last name ain't Vida!" was all he said as he snatched the dog out my hand and went back into the house.

The neighborhood never saw much of Ms. Darlene's husband, but when we did it was always a show and never a good one. Each time, all the kids started talking about it and causing discomfort in their homes. They would casually bring up at dinner tables, "Ms. Darlene's husband said *insert expletive* today," and at grocery store errands, "Ms. Darlene's husband came outside yesterday. He didn't have a shirt on and smelled like pee-

pee."

About three years later, Ms. Darlene had a son. Well, she fostered one and he was about a year older than I was, so we played together sometimes. His name was Keanu and he never got along with Ms. Darlene's husband (but then again, no one did). He rang our doorbell once and asked if I could play.

"Be back before it gets dark," my mom told me in a way that I knew meant she wasn't completely on board with the idea.

Keanu and I walked down the block in silence.

"Umm…where are we going?" I asked once we reached the corner.

"To see something cool."

He kept walking and I followed. We walked about two more blocks and reached the community park, which was pretty empty since it was the end of September and starting to get darker earlier. I followed him behind some shrubbery, and he pulled out something from the dirt. I didn't know what it was until he aimed it at me.

"Whoa! What are you doing!?" I jumped back.

"Relax, I'm not going to shoot you!"

He laughed at me.

"Where did you even get that?"

He shrugged, "I found it."

Keanu didn't live with Ms. Darlene for very long. All our parents talked about it amongst each other, but never to the kids.

Over the years, Ms. Darlene had lost her husband, then

Darwin. Her husband died from something alcohol related. (Go to South Lake if you want to hear some entertaining stories about what exactly happened). Most of the kids had gotten older and moved and the ones who stayed brought a new generation in to know who Ms. Darlene was. It wasn't until my own mother had passed that I found myself back in the neighborhood and at her porch.

"Hi, Ms. Darlene,"

"Oh, hi honey!" she said with the kind of warmth that only comes from the Ms. Darlenes of the world.

She invited me into her house and offered me cookies and milk, just like I was one of the neighborhood kids again.

"I'm sorry about your mother. She was a very good woman," she said void of the staleness that the cliché usually holds.

"Thanks," I said and grabbed a cookie.

"You know, I've seen so many things happen in this neighborhood and I'm surprised I have lived to see it all," she said.

"You've lived here all your life, haven't you?"

"Yes, I have."

"Have you ever thought about moving? You know, maybe live in some other part of the world?"

"Oh, honey no. I've seen all I've needed to see. After my husband died, I went to Florida. I got my passport and went to Brazil and Greece. I went jet skiing and I even went skydiving with my sister."

"What? You went skydiving?"

She laughed.

"You think an old woman like me can't go skydiving?"

We both laughed. She relaxed back in her chair and folded her hands in her lap.

"A lot of people felt sorry for me after that man died, but you want to know something? I didn't feel bad about it at all. Once that man drank himself to his own grave, I finally got to do what I wanted to do. I still do sometimes, and I love coming back to this house. It's always been home to me."

We talked about her husband and Keanu and Darwin and a lot of other things I never knew about her. That was the first and last real conversation I had with Ms. Darlene. She passed away a few years after that. And although there's a new family living at 2135, it will always be Ms. Darlene's house.

RUBY STALLION

Shampoo dripped into his eyes making them burn but he didn't care. He just had to get the smell of her off his skin. The 'Ruby Stallion' perfume was potent and distinguishable, like frankincense and wild orange. It used to intoxicate him to a high beyond any drug he would take. Good thing Sienna wasn't home. If she'd so much as caught a whiff of him, she'd know what happened and walk right out the door. She'd given him a second chance before and she made it clear that a third wasn't in the cards. He watched the water and soap drip from his arms down to his fingers and fixated on the tattoo on his ring finger...Sienna had the same one. And in a weird twisted way, it was because of that tattoo and the reason behind it that caused him to get in-volved with HER.

~

Carman. Her hair was long, wild, and dyed jet black. But she was the only one who could pull it off. She danced off beat to the music and didn't care who was watching. In the crowded nightclub, most people weren't, but Salem had his eye on her. He looked barely old enough to legally take a drink, even though he was significantly older. He'd made up for it in muscle. That was his in with her. He'd sat at the bar and held his drink in his hand like some shy college kid, tuning everyone else as he watched her. She was met with multiple men on the dance floor asking her to dance and she turned every one of them down. It was like each man saw the increasing challenge and wanted to prove himself worthy. Salem didn't dare go over there. He knew that he wasn't what she was interested in. Still...it didn't stop him from watching her.

Finally, one guy came up that she decided to give the actual time of day. He was a bit older than her. Salem watched as he swayed, and she sashayed. He was awkward, but she flowed with elegance and temptation in a hypnotic way that was harmful but intoxicating. Like a sailor drawn to the call of a Siren. Salem kept his focus. Carman began to explore the man's body with her hands, and it made Salem uncomfortable, but he tried to keep his cool. She turned to face the man. Her fingertips searched his waist. Up to his chest. Then, slowly, back down again until she was at his legs. And back up again. Then back down again. She rested her hands at his belt loops while she turned up the dancing. Salem's eyes were glued to her. The music and the people in the room didn't matter anymore. She was all he saw. He gulped his beer to calm his nerves.

Her fingers trailed to the man's pants pockets and Salem knew he couldn't waste any more time. He took the biggest swig of beer he could and confidently made his way to the dance floor. In five seconds, he was standing next to the man.

"Excuse me sir, can I cut in?" he asked politely.

"No! Get your own girl!"

"It's ok. I don't mind." Those were the first words she'd spoken all night. She sounded different than Salem thought she would; more innocence to her voice.

"I said no!" the man said, obviously drunk, and shoved Salem.

Salem, although probably almost half his age, was twice his muscle. He pushed the man back and he stumbled back a bit. He gained his footing before falling and ran to him, swinging his fist in the air, ready to throw a punch at him. He missed and Salem threw one back, but tried not to give all his force. He didn't want to seriously injure the man. Before he knew it, they were tussling on the floor. The music stopped and in a swift moment, security had them both by the arms. It all happened in less than a minute. "Both of you get out!" he heard one of the security guards yell. Before he could even try and leave on his own, he was being escorted out by two security guards through a back door. The old man was being escorted out the front. They left him outside in the dark and slammed the door behind him. Instead of going home, he pulled a cigarette out of his pocket and lit it, smoking as he waited. He was halfway through his cigarette when she came out the back door.

"You got what you came for?" he asked her, motioning to her pocket that contained the wallet they both knew was there. But they both also knew she didn't dare take it out now.

"Salem." she reached out and gave him a hug, running her palm through her hair, leaving that trace of *Ruby Stallion*. It was her way of 'reading the mind'.

"Good to see you're standing...and your thinking is straight." Carman wasn't sentimental and she wasn't being that way now. The innocent routine she displayed in the club was gone. It was one thing Salem liked about what they had.

"Any cash?" he asked to keep his mind on the business and not on whether or not Sienna had made it home.

"You still think too small." She poked at his head. Cash lasts the weekend. Everything else in here can last a decade if you use it right," she patted at her pocket.

"Who asked you for it this time?"

"Ex-girlfriend. Typical."

"So what? We just use his license to--"

"Shhhh..." she brought her finger to her mouth, "you want too many answers too soon. This isn't as cut and dry as what we used to do. It takes time for longer results."

"It's been a minute since we worked together. Sorry if I'm a little rusty."

"It's ok. I know Sienna isn't warm to it," she chuckled, "This is why I don't fall in love. It's bad for business."

Salem didn't respond to her...because he knew there was some truth to it. If people were in love, or even just showed love more, he might be out of work. And then what would he tell Sienna? He'd already been covering up the fact that he'd been fired from his real job for two months. After that last check came, he knew he'd have to come up with another way to make money.

The night wouldn't end in passion, or a night together, or even so much as a kiss between Salem and Carman. Carman wasn't into men...or women either for that matter. And Salem only had romantic eyes for Sienna. What they had in common was their addiction to the adrenaline. An addiction that put his relationship with Sienna at risk every night he did this, but Carman's business had no signs of slowing down any time soon, so neither would he.

"Go home to your wife, Salem. I'll text you for the next step."

"What exactly is the next step?"

"You'll find out when you show up."

Salem shrugged and began to walk towards his car. He knew better than to offer to escort Carman to hers.

"Hey! It'll be next week. I'll have your financial cut too."

"Thanks, Carm."

She waved him off and they parted.

~

"Care for company?"

Salem's thoughts were interrupted by Sienna joining him in the shower.

"Sure, babe. I missed you."

He grabbed her hands that were wrapped around his waist and brought them to his lips to kiss them.

"I know. I missed you too. Can't wait to be done with these later shifts."

"You're helping sick people. It's ok. Just wish I didn't have to share you with them sometimes."

They both laughed.

"Was your day ok?"

He paused.

"Yeah...uneventful. Just happy to be home with you."

He kissed her forehead. She smiled and he did too. Half because he was happy to be near her, and half because she hadn't smelled any trace of the Ruby Stallion.

SOMETIMES THEY SAY NOTHING

"I'm not good enough for you."

"Well, what do you mean?"

"I'm not good enough for you," he repeated. My 15-year-old brain didn't comprehend what he really meant. Gary was a senior and, in my world, that meant he was infinitely more mature...and infinitely more important than anything else in my life. He'd taken me to our favorite ice cream shop and ordered my favorite chocolate ice cream on a waffle cone.

"So, I've been meaning to talk to you," he started as soon as we sat down on the wooden bench outside. He didn't have any ice cream, which was odd, but I didn't think anything of it. Here he was, acting like a subpar father, trying to bribe his kids with ice cream to make up for his shortcomings.

"Yeah, sure. What's up?" I asked, not looking at him or thinking of what this conversation would entail. In a lot of ways, I was still a kid at heart, so my focus was mainly on my ice cream.

"I think we should break up."

"What?!" I said, absentmindedly dropping my ice cream on my white mini skirt. He grabbed a napkin and tried to help me wipe it off, but it did nothing to hide the big hideous brown stain that I was never able to get out.

"Why? What did I do?" I asked.

"It's nothing you did. You're just such a good girl. It's just…
I'm not good enough for you."

～

"It's what's best."

"You've got that right!"

I was saying one thing, but internally, I couldn't disagree more. But there was a part of me that considered that maybe he was right. After all, he was kind of a joke. I didn't owe him anything. I hadn't seen him since I was nine years old and it had now been over ten years. If anything, he owed me way more than a half-hearted explanation. He owed me more than this rushed farse of a reunion on my college campus. We sat in the quad, delicately being caressed by the mist from the fountain. Ordinarily, it felt amazing on my skin. But today, not so much.

Great, Dad. Now I'll never be able to enjoy the fountain again.

Our awkward time together had quickly escalated to an

argument after I cut right to the chase and asked, "Will you ever come back and try to make things better? Even if not with mom, with me and Nico?"

"I don't think so, Noni."

He didn't even think about his response. His quick, blunt answer took me aback so much, that I reactively boomeranged his response only with more volume, drawing the attention of the other young adults studying nearby.

"What do you mean?! You don't think you owe us at least that?! Why not?!"

"It's what's best."

~

"I need to focus on myself."

"And you can't focus on yourself with me around?" he scoffed at me.

He was my best friend all throughout college and we finally decided to take the next step to a relationship. But lately, I'd felt my feelings start to diminish. And I had no desire to rekindle it. Ironically, I'd taken him out for ice cream like Gary had done to me five years before then. Logan was the only person who loved ice cream as much as me, so I hoped this would numb the sting I was about to deliver him rather than make him hate ice cream forever.

"So, I've been meaning to talk to you," I said, feeling the déjà vu of my own ice cream heartbreak.

"Oh, yeah! How'd it go with your father," he asked as he scooped ice cream out his cup. I looked out the campus buffet window, the sun was glistening abnormally bright and I shielded my eyes and looked back at him.

"Terribly. But that's not what I want to talk to you about."

"Oh...Ok then. What's up?"

I took a deep breath. It was my first time initiating a face-to-face breakup.

"You know how I feel about you," I grabbed his hand from across the table, "but I think I need some space."

"What do you mean space?" he made the word seem dirty.

"I just have to figure some things out."

"But haven't I been giving you space? You asked me to wait before bringing up your dad. We haven't hung out in a few days so you could think. Whenever you're distant and want to be alone, I back off. What did I do wrong?"

You didn't do anything. It's not you-"

"Please tell me you're not going to say, 'It's not you it's me?'"

Was I really sounding like a walking cliché right now? He pulled his hand away.

"Noni, are you breaking up with me?"

I shook my head yes, avoiding eye contact and watching

my own hand stir the melting ice cream. I briefly glanced at his face, watching him visibly try and swallow the knot in his throat. I was doing this to him, and I felt bad enough to empathize, but not bad enough to stop the words from coming out my mouth:

"I need to focus on myself."

~

Our relationship has run its course.

"You're joking, right?"

Shortly after breaking up with Logan, my roommate, who was also my best friend, Pamela decided to move out. Granted, I hadn't exactly been the nicest to her either. I rarely cleaned up after myself and stayed up at night loudly playing music when I knew she had to work early in the morning. Whenever she'd call me on it, I would irrationally blow up at her, "No one says anything when your boyfriend comes over and eats our food!" Her boyfriend had only accidentally eaten my food once, thinking it was hers, but I still used it to get her off my back.

I came home one day after leaving my night class early and saw her wheeling her suitcase toward the door. "Where are you going? Seeing your parents early this weekend?" I asked her.

"Noni!" My presence had obviously surprised her, "I wasn't expecting you until after 9."

"Class got out an hour early."

"Oh. Well, I was going to leave you a note," she pointed to the refrigerator that had a white folded piece of paper taped to it.

"What's it about?" I asked, ignoring the note and opening the refrigerator for a snack.

"Ummm...I...uh...I think it's best if I stay with Doug for a while."

"Why?" I asked, not realizing what she was saying yet.

"Well...we haven't really been getting along." Pamela was the non-confrontational type, so it was no surprise that she was struggling to get the words out.

"How long will you stay there then? For the weekend?" She scratched her head, "Uh...no. I...uh. I'm moving out.

"What?!"

"Noni, I'm sorry, but I just don't think this is working. Not just us living together, but us being friends."

Instead of blowing up at her, I felt the warm tears on my face before I even noticed they were falling.

"Pam, please. I know I haven't been the greatest lately but let me fix it. I... I'll stop playing music loudly. I'll start cleaning up after myself. I'll stop yelling at you," I tried to take the suitcase out her hand, but she grabbed it closer to herself. I was crying at that point, more than I had for any breakup with any guy.

"Pamela, no," I stamped my foot, "I really need you right now. I need my friend."

I looked in her eyes in search of some kind of sign she'd

change her mind. But instead, I just saw foggy eyes that were upset and tired and... done.

"Our relationship has run its course."

$$\sim$$

Sometimes they say nothing.

"No, I won the bumper cars! Did you see how hard I hit you?"

"You cheated!"

"You can't cheat at bumper cars!"

My mom, my brother Nico and I had come home from a day at the arcade. My mother had been tuning us out the entire ride home, but once we got in the house, her patience had all but run out of listening to our playful banter.

"Kids, please!"

We stopped yelling so loudly and went down to a kid's version of a whisper.

"You cheated."

"No, I didn't."

"Noni! Go upstairs and see if your father is still taking a nap. It's almost time for dinner."

I went upstairs, still whispering, "You cheated," hoping Nico heard me. There was a rule in our house. If one of my parents were sleeping or resting, we were to be extra quiet especially when coming up the stairs. It was like a stealth mission danger zone. I peeked in my parents' room and he wasn't in there, so I went to his study, where he usually went after a nap, but he wasn't there either. In fact, none of his things were there. The room was completely empty, devoid of all his books, his desktop, and his files. The only thing left was a table and an empty bookcase.

"Mom!!" I yelled.

She ran up the stairs and met me in the study.

"I think we've been robbed!" I told her. She didn't say anything. But the look on her face said more than my nine-year-old brain could comprehend. I saw the tears well up in her eyes as she stared at the empty room. As a tear silently trickled down her cheek, she quickly wiped it away. I pretended not to notice and grabbed her hand. She brought our intertwined hands to her lips and kissed mine. Then released it and went to her bedroom and closed the door.

And I realized much later that sometimes it's not even the words. Sometimes their choice to love has changed and clichés come to soften the blow. And when that isn't sufficient, there are no words at all. And sometimes...

Sometimes they say nothing.